Merry and Moon

Potion Commotion

T. Lockhaven

WITH S.T. WHITE

TWISTED KEY
publishing

2021

First Printing: 2021

ISBN 978-1-63911-001-8

Twisted Key Publishing, LLC
www.twistedkeypublishing.com

Ordering Information:
Special discounts are available on quantity purchases by corporations, associations, educators, and others. For details, contact the publisher at the above listed address.

U.S. trade bookstores and wholesalers: Please contact Twisted Key Publishing, LLC by email twistedkeypublishing@gmail.com.

Acknowledgements

Special thanks to S.T. White for collaborating with us on this story. It's been so much fun bringing these characters to life and building such a magical world.

We also wanted to thank our editor team and beta readers—Elisabeth Allen, Nikki Boccelli-Saltsman and Christine Mattila—for all the helpful feedback and suggestions.

Contents

1 - Merry

The brew was nearly complete, all that it needed was the tail of a purple newt, and a drop of pure blood. Gwynevere Merry furrowed her brow confused by the lack of substantial color change to the lime green mix. She slid the old witch's recipe book across the table and ran her finger down the list of ingredients. Each word was etched into the paper with the sharp pen strokes of her mother's handwriting, which made her writing tangible to the touch. "Aha!" she exclaimed as she came upon the missing ingredient. "A dash of rat whiskers...?"

A panicked squeaking ensued as her eyes casually glanced up to see her pet familiar, an albino rat, staring at her from beside the small, boiling cauldron. She smirked as she set the book down and held her hand out for her furry friend.

"It's just a manner of witch speak, Samuel," she reassured her rat familiar. She picked him up to let him perch on her shoulder. "A dash of rat whiskers is like a code word, but for what...?"

Her eyes scanned the room. She knew her mother wouldn't have tasked her with making such a brew without giving her the ingredients she needed. After all, how is a witch's apprentice supposed to learn without access to all her tools? Gwynevere flicked her razor-sharp teeth with her tongue as she pondered. Her eyes fell upon a small clay pot growing a common weed.

"Arabidopsis!" she cried as she threw her hands up in the air. "Of course! The lab rat of all plants!" Samuel held on to the fabric of Gwynevere's long black dress to keep from being tossed off in her excitement. He squeaked in offense once more before crawling up the back of her neck, through her long locks of silver white hair, and under her tall, pointy witch hat. He then poked his head out from under the frill and twitched his whiskers.

"Oh Samuel, come off it," said Gwynevere. She plucked a few small twig-sized pieces of the weed stem. "I swear, you're so dramatic, I'd think you were offended on purpose."

She dropped the stems into the brew. It huffed a plume of green smoke that turned purple mid-burst. She danced and clapped her hands happily. "Success!" she cried.

She slipped on a pair of oven mitts and grabbed the cast iron handles attached to the old brewing cauldron. She lifted it and grunted at its weight, doing her best not to trip as she hurried out the door of the small cottage shack where she worked. The outdoor air was cool with the nip of fall, and the crunch of fallen leaves beneath her feet filled Gwynevere with a sense of relief. She was happy to be out of the tiny workspace, toiling away for hours, to make this brew.

She hurried through the open forest which served as the backyard to a massive gothic manor. The chipper girl pushed through the backdoor straight into the kitchen where she could hear her mother and father yelling at each other halfway through the house. "If that were the case I would have been out of here a long time ago!" she heard her mother cry from the foyer.

"You're only here because of your daughter and not because of me!" shouted her father. "I wish you could look me in the eyes and just say it!"

It was the same old song and dance again. Gwynevere sighed. She bustled into the kitchen and set the bubbling brew on the counter next to the sink and pulled off her mitts. For as long as she could remember, her parents never got along. Her father was a vampire and an important judge on the council of the city of Ashen. Her mother was a renowned potion brewer and a teacher at the Ashen Academy. She had been working with Gwynevere to prepare her for the day she turned sixteen and could apply for a brewing scholarship at the academy.

The door opened as her mother walked in and looked at her. "By Grimlock's beard." The sight of her daughter seemed to startle her. "I thought you would still be out in the brewing cabin."

"I finished," said Gwynevere proudly.

She knew better than to mention anything about her parents fighting. She watched her mother curiously approach the cauldron and stare at the bubbling lavender-colored contents. She dipped her finger in the brew, pulled it back and tasted it. She raised a brow and smiled at her daughter with gleaming delight. Gwynevere blinked and smiled innocently at her. "Yes, Mother?" she chirped.

"My dear, I think you may have just concocted the perfect brew!" said her mother, obviously delighted at her daughter's success.

Now Gwynevere knew it was time to ask her mom the burning question. "Great! So, what does it do?"

Samuel popped his curious little head from the rim of her hat. Her mother eyed the little rat then looked back at her daughter and waved a finger. "All in due time," she said. "It is but a *piece* of what may be my greatest achievement since having you."

"Does Mama Maggie know about this?" asked Gwynevere.

"Since when does she have to know about anything?" her mother retorted. "She claimed the title of a sombre witch and since then she believed herself to be above anybody and anything." She huffed with a disgruntled grimace on her face. "If there is one thing you should always count on, it is that that woman will do whatever it takes to serve herself first."

Gwynevere looked at her mother and tilted her head. "Are you and Mama Maggie fighting again?" she asked.

Her mother paused and looked over at her, releasing a slow sigh. "It's nothing you should have to concern yourself with, dear."

Gwynevere nodded and shrugged. Her mother picked up the cauldron and hauled it over to a massive mixing pot and poured the potion into it.

She had heard her mother use the term *sombre* witch before. It was a classification of natural-born talented witches that essentially had the full extent of their potential tapped into all branches of magic. Once upon a time they were considered supreme witches, but progressive times had changed. Now witches were content with focusing on only one or two subjects of magic they wished to perfect. Gwynevere was barely able to manage simple spellcasting, let alone potion brewing. However, her mother continued to encourage her. She flicked her sharp fangs in frustration, wishing for once that her mother would just tell her something outright. She knew better than to probe her for further information though, especially when she wanted it to be a surprise.

"Is there anything else, Mom?" she asked, standing there, anxious about her parents fighting again, among several other things.

"I think your father wanted to speak to you, dear," she said without turning away from the brew. "He's upstairs, brooding as usual."

"Yes, ma'am." Gwynevere let out a heavy sigh. "Come, Samuel, off on another boring adventure."

Gwynevere's mother turned and watched her daughter leave for the main hall. Her crystal blue eyes stared unwavering, until she was out of sight. She returned to the brew, pulling from various jars of glowing liquid and dumping their contents into the large iron pot, creating multiple bright plumes of smoke, all the while chanting in an ancient tongue.

She knew her daughter would find out soon enough how talented a witch she truly was. She had the natural gift of magic. Even as a child she could make objects move and light fires with a simple thought. Powerful for a child so young. A heavy pain filled her heart. If only she knew how to tell her how proud she was.

Gwynevere approached the long, winding stairs at the heart of the manor. "It's no wonder guests don't like to visit," she said to Samuel who agreed with a simple little squeak. He slipped back under his master's hat as she made her way up the stairs and down the dark hall to her father's room. Unlike her,

her father was completely adverse to the light, not having any of the strengths of human blood to counter the wickedness that was the sun. She opened the door to his chambers and found him staring at one of his paintings, his arms crossed over his chest. "Mom said you wanted to see me…?"

He turned and looked at her with a gentle smile that revealed his razor-sharp, matured teeth. "My child, please, come in," he said in his soft yet heavy voice.

Gwynevere approached her father and smiled softly. She always found him more fascinating than intimidating, though his demeanor often made his behavior unpredictable which set Gwynevere on edge, despite knowing she had nothing to fear in his presence.

She turned to look at the painting he seemed so keenly focused on, only to see herself staring right back at her. It was a family portrait, capturing a time when her parents seemed happier. Her father smiling with his teeth shown proudly, wearing his finest suit. Her mother stood beside him, holding baby Gwynevere in her arms, her child-like eyes beaming wide with excitement at whatever it was the artist did to grab her attention.

"You were such a beautiful child," he said to her. "Platinum white hair, big ruby eyes, little razors already coming in. You were without a doubt a Merry just from the look of you."

"Mom always said I favored you," said Gwynevere, wondering what her parents' fight was about to make him act in such a way.

"That is a lie," he said. "Aside from those traits you're a spitting image of your mother in every way. Your soft features give off a sense of innocence."

He looked back at Gwynevere. "You've grown to become a beautiful young woman," he said proudly. He reached into his pocket and pulled out his watch to check the time. "My dear, have I ever told you about the Sanguines Drop?"

Her eyes fluttered, racing through her memories of all the things she might have learned in the past. "N-no? I don't think so, Father," she replied.

"Hmm… curious." He walked over toward her and placed his hand gently on her shoulder. "It is a vessel of ancient making, said to preserve the blood of a treasured loved one."

"Is this the start of one of those romantic pick-up lines you use to apologize for yelling at Mom?" asked Gwynevere rather plainly.

"What? No, it—" He stopped himself mid-sentence and looked back at Gwynevere. For the time, he decided it was best just to drop it. "It will still be light for a couple more hours. I need you to deliver a letter for me, to the city council." He gestured to a letter laying on his desk, wrapped in red ribbon and stamped with the house crest of Merry. "Take it to the Mayor please, dear. It's urgent he has it before nightfall."

"You want to get your first words in before Judge Aiden has her say?" asked Gwynevere, aware her father was often competitive with his fellow council judge and vampire.

"Judge Aiden couldn't pass a ruling in a fortnight, much less before sundown," her father chuckled. "Still, if you do see her... tell her I wish her well for me. We've not had much of a chance for any sort of private exchanges in some time."

"Sure," Gwynevere smiled, "I'll deliver it right away."

It wasn't often he put his trust in her to do anything, so she was ready and willing to help. Even though the weather was overcast and cloudy, she knew her father couldn't risk being outside—that is, without dressing in such a way that it could, as he put it, cost him dignity. Still, it gave her a sense of pride to be needed, even for such a menial task. She hurried down the stairs and back toward the kitchen. "I'm running into town, Mom!" she called to her.

There was a prolonged silence before she heard a response. "Okay, honey, be careful!" she called back.

Gwynevere adjusted her hat and headed out the front door, walking along the stone path that led into the large, sprawling city of Ashen.

2 - Moody

"Another box for the back stock, Father," said Evelyn Moody as she brought in another crate from the wagon and set it down on the counter next to her father.

He slid his reading glasses down his nose and casually peered at the box's contents. "No, that's the tanned leather for the shoes." He grabbed it and placed it down next to him behind the counter.

"Shoes?" asked Evelyn. She wiped her brow with her sleeve. "Since when are you a cobbler?"

"Since Mrs. Baker down the street started selling shoes and tripling her stock," her father responded very matter-of-factly. He tapped a pencil on a sheet of parchment, and then turned to his daughter. "Come around here," he motioned, "and take off your shoes."

Evelyn raised a brow and slipped around the counter. Her father laid the parchment on the floor and looked up at her. Evelyn wanted to scream, but she knew she couldn't simply deny her father from venturing off into new territory. That was just the way he operated. She also knew it was in both of their best interests to humor him. Evelyn slid off her muddy boots and stepped barefoot onto the paper. She watched her father trace an outline around her feet.

Evelyn sighed and half-smiled. "You know, you don't have to try and do everything."

"Why not?" he tapped her ankle, motioning for her to step off the paper.

Her father picked up a strip of leather and studied it thoroughly. Evelyn could tell he didn't know the first thing about making shoes, but she admired him for never doubting himself.

"Hey, uhm," she started to speak, mostly to see if she could get his attention away from his new sudden fascination. "Do you mind getting the last load of linens off the wagon? I'd like to go clean up."

Her father did not move his gaze but nodded. "Go ahead, sweetheart. You've worked hard enough today," he said gently.

Evelyn sighed with relief. She crossed the room and paused at the foot of the stairs that ran along the back wall of the tailor shop, to the living quarters. Her legs felt like cement columns as she lumbered across the room. She looked at her bed and moaned, *if only I could just collapse.* She was greeted with a soft meow. She knelt to pet the black cat as he lovingly rubbed against her legs.

"Hey, Rufus. You must be hungry," she said, as she scratched behind his ears.

Rufus responded with a resounding meow. He followed his master across the room to a small barrel where she pulled out the only remaining dried horse meat. "Looks like Father had to make cuts on spending again." She sat the salted meat on the floor in front of the starving cat. "Make this last if you can," she smiled.

Rufus responded with a happy purr. While he ate, Evelyn shuffled to the washroom, chastising herself with each step. *I feel like I'm a hundred years old.* She drew back the curtain and looked at the wash basin and the ancient water pump. It had been nearly a week since she last cleaned up, typical for the times as her father reminded her often that the water basin was a luxury they shouldn't have been able to afford. She stared at the pump for a long time, focusing on the handle until a spark glistened in her crystal blue eyes. The pump started to slowly move up and down, pumping well water into the basin. Evelyn smirked with satisfaction. She padded over to the dirty old mirror behind the sink.

"Eesh, Evelyn, you *look* like you're a hundred years old," she said aloud. A meow of agreement came from the other room. "Hey, watch it mister," she laughed, "don't forget where that delicious horse meat comes from."

Evelyn unknotted the bun that held her long black hair atop her head, and let it fall to her waist. She tilted her head from side to side stretching her neck. The basin was nearly filled. She rolled up a sleeve, letting the water splash on her hand. The water was warm today, almost warm enough to enjoy. She smiled, excited to actually have a moment of privacy. Suddenly something caught her eye, a flicker or shadow reflected in the mirror.

"Hey!" she shouted as she hurried out of the washroom and looked around the room. "Dad?"

There was no one there. Confused, she walked around the sparsely furnished room, checking everything just to be sure, including looking under both beds. She looked back to Rufus who licked his lips happily from a full meal. "No wonder you're getting so fat," she laughed as she walked back to the washroom. *It must have been my imagination.* "Hey Rufus. Keep a look out for suspicious shadows."

Rufus meowed, *okay*, and then plunked onto his side and stretched. "Worst watch cat ever," Evelyn sighed, closing the curtains once more.

Nearly an hour passed, and the day turned to dusk. The orange and red sky was visible through the single window inside the living quarters. Rufus had repositioned himself on the windowsill, luxuriating in the last warm rays of sunlight. Evelyn stepped out of the washroom feeling renewed, dressed in a far more comfortable long white dress and stockings. She slowly brushed through her wet hair and laughed at her lazy cat.

"Oh, Rufus. Ever the vigilante watchdog," she said with a sigh. Rufus meowed indignantly and stretched, looking put off by her remark. Evelyn smirked. "Right, right, watch *cat*, my utmost apologies."

With that, Evelyn slipped on some comfortable shoes and walked downstairs to find her father cutting the leather. He was so focused on his task that the point of his tongue was visible through his clenched lips and bushy whiskers. She brushed her hair back from her face and cleared her throat, causing him to look up from his work and smile.

"Well don't you look beautiful?" he said. "As always, of course."

"Thank you, Father," Evelyn curtsied. She glanced down at her feet and then back to her dad. "I know it's late, but I was hoping I could run into town before Miss Bigsby closes for the night." She paused trying to recall the best reason to give for her outing. "Rufus is out of food and looking at me pitifully."

Her father raised a brow and looked at her over his reading glasses. "Isn't it getting late?"

"It'll be just a quick stop, Father," said Evelyn. "I'm sure I'll be back long before you've figured out how to make a shoe."

Her father smiled and looked down at his work. "Right, just be quick," he said. "You can have the coin from the register. Just buy what we need and nothing more, understand?"

"Yes, Father…," said Evelyn with a nod, relieved he actually said yes. She opened the register and grabbed just a few coins from the small pile, knowing exactly how much she needed. Rufus meowed as he approached her. She held out her hand and he leapt effortlessly into her arms.

"Oh and take Rufus with you."

"Right… because he'll protect me from any wrongdoers. Won't you little fellow?" she beamed, scratching behind his ears.

"You and that cat," he chuckled and waved his hand to her. "Go on now, before I change my mind."

"Thank you, Father," said Evelyn. She hurried to the front door, a mere second away from freedom, when her father called out to her.

"Oh, and Evelyn…," he said looking up from his hand-drawn pattern. She stopped and looked back at him with her hand already on the doorknob. "Please try to restrain yourself from any more *public* displays."

Evelyn felt her cheeks blush. She sighed and nodded. "Yes, Father… again, sorry about that."

With permission granted, she swung open the door and darted out into the evening air, hurrying across their yard toward the town of Yorkshire, the only place the young girl had ever known. A gust of wind blew across the path, it was crisp and cool. Evelyn breathed in deeply, a fresh relief from the warm summer day.

Yorkshire was a bit peculiar. At this hour, there were hardly any people out and about. The locals turned in early, and most of the businesses shut down at the first hint of nightfall. It was as if the town was controlled by a timer. The townsfolk were a bit odd too, keeping mostly to themselves.

Rufus meowed and wove in between her legs as she walked. "Ugh, you don't have to remind me. I don't need two fathers."

Rufus meowed again in disagreement, flicking his tail to accentuate his statement.

"Look," she reassured him. "Lighting the tree on fire was a one-time accident and nobody saw it was me who started it." Rufus meowed again in a much lower, disappointed tone. "I was trying to fix the streetlamp from dying out." Rufus narrowed his eyes at her and shook his head, making a low guttural sound in his throat. "Don't you dare use that kind of language. I swear, you're just as naggy as Father."

Evelyn picked up Rufus and hurried into the main part of the town. It was filled with an assortment of shops, local government buildings, churches and homes of the well-to-do. She waved to a group of dairy workers, who were just leaving the city hall. They passed by with waves except for one man that broke from the group.

"Good evening, Ms. Moody! Is your father still selling those linen pants? I'm thinking I'm in need of at least three more pairs. An extra for me, and two for the wife," he laughed conspiratorially.

"Ha ha. Yes, I think he still has plenty," said Evelyn. She wasn't sure when the last person had come to her father's shop for new clothes. The business had been running its course, selling the same product to the same people for so many years it was hardly a profitable endeavor. Rufus started to fidget against her arm, always the antsy little bugger. "We're almost there, take it easy, I'm not a pin cushion."

She eyed the spice stand where Miss Bigsby was fixing to close up shop. The fair farmer merchant adjusted her bonnet as she watched the young girl skip up to her stand. She smiled a warm smile that radiated a lot more life and friendliness than what Evelyn often saw in Yorkshire. She was Evelyn's favorite person to talk to, as she would often poke her with questions that made her feel like she was somewhat interested in her life. She was the perfect age of interest for her father, and Evelyn suspected she might have had some interest in him, romantically. "Miss Moody, out late again I see,"

Miss Bigsby smiled. "Who's your friend?" She nodded at Rufus, who was currently nestled in Evelyn's arms.

"Oh, this is Rufus, my watch cat," Evelyn winked. "Father had me bring him along to protect me from evildoers."

"Smart man, your father," Miss Bigsby nodded.

"I suppose," Evelyn laughed. "He seems to think so." She set the coins in front of Miss Bigsby. "I wanted to know if you had any more meat left."

Miss Bigsby shook her head. "Sorry dear, food shortages and all, I don't carry the stock I would normally carry. Been having a bit of a problem with infestations as of late. Spoils a lot of good food. No good for selling, as you can imagine."

Rufus whined and Evelyn stroked his head in comfort. "I'm sorry, little man, maybe tomorrow," she said with a sigh. "Oh yes!" she exclaimed remembering the other reason she had come. "Do you have any more mustard seeds and sage? Possibly could go for another ginger root as well."

"Of course," she turned toward a series of troughs and began removing the spices, placing them into separate sacks. "Rufus… wasn't that the name of the first cat your family had?" she inquired. "I could have sworn I remember a time your father had such a thing sitting by his side in the shop. You were just a little thing then."

"Oh no, Rufus has been in the family the whole time," Evelyn confirmed with a very matter-of-fact nod.

"Really…?" Miss Bigsby looked at her with surprise. She handed the bags of spice to Evelyn who took it graciously. "How old are you now, Evelyn?"

"Sixteen," she said with a smile, handing her a couple coins. "Seventeen come winter."

"That's an awfully long-lived cat then," Miss Bigsby noted as she looked at Rufus who simply yawned and nestled into his master's arm.

Evelyn shrugged. "I guess he's just really healthy," she smiled nonchalantly.

"Yes, I'm sure, and your father, how is he?" she asked with a bit more perk in her lip.

"Tiring away at his next big idea," said Evelyn. "It's not like there is much else to do in this town. Maybe you should come by some time. He's been wanting to practice shoemaking. He'd probably be grateful for an adult's help."

Miss Bigsby caught the not-so-very-subtle wink that followed the young girl's words. She chuckled and covered her mouth. "Oh my," she blushed, "perhaps one day soon," she said.

"Well, I best be going now," said Evelyn, picking up the bags filled with spice. "Have a wonderful evening. Thank you!" She called out over her shoulder.

"Thank you, dear," said Miss Bigsby. She stroked her chin as Evelyn hurried away. "Most curious...."

Evelyn rushed toward her home. The sun had set, and the city watch were busily lighting the streetlamps. She hummed on her journey down the winding cobblestone path, that led to their shop, holding Rufus in one arm and twirling her sacks of spices in the other.

"Once Father is asleep, you and I will have another go at that brew," she told Rufus as she passed beneath a glowing streetlamp. That was when something caught her eye in the distance. A sudden shuffling in the brush and the movement of a shadow. She paused and looked out into the darkness beyond the small wall that separated the road from the farmland. "Hello? Someone there?"

Rufus sensed something was amiss. He growled and hopped out of Evelyn's arm. "Rufus? What do you see?" she asked, her voice filled with worry. Rufus's fur stood on end, and he arched his back, a low growl rumbled in the back of his throat. "What is it?"

The snap of a twig startled them both. Her heart beat wildly. She scooped Rufus into her arms and began running, the bags of spices bouncing in her hand.

She reached the door and stumbled inside. Her father was still working at his desk, etching new markings along the paper. He looked up at her, noticing her pale complexion. "Evelyn? Is something wrong?" he asked, a worried look on his face.

Evelyn quickly hid the sacks, tucking them under Rufus who was still cradled in her arms. "Oh? No, nothing," she said in a huff. "Just heard something walking back and got startled is all. It gets a little spooky out there at night."

"I see…," her father twitched his mustache, ever suspicious of his daughter who was known for her bouts of mischievousness. "Did you find what you were looking for? What was it, food for the cat?"

"Yes, and the pudgy bugger ate it while Miss Bigsby and I had a chat," Evelyn lied. She walked to the back of the shop and paused at the foot of the stairs. Guilt danced around in her head and her heart. "I'm heading up… don't stay up too late for a change, please."

"I'll try not to," he said with a light chuckle.

"I love you, Father."

"I love you too, Evelyn."

She smiled softly at him as the crystal in her eyes sparkled in the lamplight. After a moment, she turned and headed upstairs, having had quite enough of startling noises and elusive shadows for one day.

3 - Silence

The letter burned a hole in Gwynevere's curiosity. *What is so urgent about the contents of this letter that it has to be delivered before nightfall?* She reached the grand, imposing doors of the city hall and waved her hand in a circular motion. The massive knob turned, and the door creaked open, just enough for Gwynevere to fit through with the wide brim of her witch's hat. She barely managed to step a foot inside when a shadow whisked out, knocking her to the ground with a startled "Oof." Gwynevere sat up and straightened her crooked hat.

"By the night, dear child, I beg your pardon!" shouted Judge Aiden.

She reached out to help the young witch up with long, pale fingers veiled in black lace, a thin gold band with a small red emerald encircled her ring finger. Gwynevere looked at the elder vampire in awe. She was dressed head to toe in black and wearing a large black veil hat to hide from the sun. What seemed off was that she was in quite the hurry. "H-hello, ma'am," she said as she took her hand and allowed the woman to help her up. "Just running a delivery. Father said—"

"I don't have time, little dhampir," said the judge. She paused and cupped her ice-cold hands over Gwynevere's cheeks. "I don't mean to be rude… you do look so much like your mother."

"T-thank you," said Gwynevere, intensely confused. Judge Aiden let go and whisked by her, tilting her hat down to hide from the sun as she hurried into the street. "Where are you going?!"

"Ashen Academy," the judge shouted back. "Where you're headed someday, no doubt."

Gwynevere smirked as Samuel popped out of her hat long enough to announce he was okay. He gave his nose a twitch and wiggle. "Yeah, I think we're supposed to like her," she said to him. She watched the judge until she disappeared from sight. "At least Father says so." That alone made her not want to shun the elder vampire's kindness. She hurried back through the doors into the city hall, the scent of hyacinth filled her nose. She fought back a sneeze and pushed through another set of large wooden doors with a golden placard that read *Clerk's Office*.

"Hi, Dolly," Gwynevere chirped, coming to a stop at the receptionist desk.

Dolly the receptionist was an animated ghoul pieced together with the body of a beautifully preserved, deceased woman. She looked like a stitched-up doll fit to be a fashion model—a real pride and joy of her masters at the council. "Gwynevere Merry? A pleasant surprise," she cooed as she leaned onto the desk and twirled her red, yarn-like hair.

"Thank you," Gwynevere smiled. "Wonderful to see you too. My father wanted me to deliver this letter to the Mayor. Said it was urgent and couldn't wait."

"I see," said the ghoul. She reached out and inspected the letter, glancing it over before setting it down on the desk. "Well, Mayor Wimbly is very busy. I'll let him know you stopped by."

"Cancel that, Dolly dear," came a booming voice behind her. Gwynevere looked up at the tall, dark man as he stepped out of his office and gently placed a hand on the ghoul's shoulder. He smirked, looking at the young witch with a snaggle-toothed grin. "You're Adonis's girl, correct?" He narrowed his eyes. "You look just like him."

"Yes, sir," said Gwynevere. It was discomforting to be in the presence of a werewolf so close to sundown. She had heard from multiple people how much she looked like both parents at this point. She was ready to be known for being herself. "Uhm, I ran into Judge Aiden." *Literally*, thought Gwynevere. "She was hurrying off to the Academy. Do you know if it was about my application?" she asked, her face filled with hope.

"Ms. Aiden's business is clearly not something she discusses with me," said the Mayor in a huff.

"I apologize," said Gwynevere, her cheeks flushing red. "It's driving me crazy, you know, the *not* knowing."

The Mayor rolled his eyes and gestured toward the letter. "Open that up for me please, dear," he said in his naturally smug-sounding voice. "By Ashen's moon, I don't have time to be a messenger boy for these night stalkers."

Gwynevere wrinkled her nose at him. Werewolves and vampires had not been known to get along, even in the most peaceful of times. Dolly nodded as she opened up the letter and handed it to the Mayor. Gwynevere's eyes widened, she'd never really paid attention to the Mayor's hands, but they were pawlike and massive. Even in their human forms, elder werewolves looked more akin to their primal selves in the right light. She'd never seen a transformed wolf in person, and she wasn't sure if she was ready *tonight* of all nights.

The massive man looked at Gwynevere with soft eyes. He rubbed the seal of the crest labeled on the letter. "Tell me, how is your mother, dear child? I haven't heard from Adelaide in some time."

"I'm, uhm, not a child, sir. I'm fifteen," Gwynevere huffed and cleared her throat. "Respectively, sir... and she's fine. She's been helping me prepare for admission to the Ashen Academy."

"Oh, that's a nice place," commented Dolly as she listened in on the conversation.

Gwynevere stood awkwardly as she watched the Mayor open the seal and read the letter. He scoffed before tucking it into his vest pocket. "Tell your father that I hope he's doing well." He spun on his heel and walked heavily toward his office.

"Yes, sir, I'll tell him," Gwynevere called out, feeling a tenseness in her chest lighten up only after he had closed the door to his office.

She turned back to Dolly, who stared at her peculiarly, like the kind of look a proud mother would stare at her child. "You look so much like your mother," she said with a smile. "Do send my regards."

"Thank you, Dolly, I will," Gwynevere replied cheerfully.

She waved goodbye to the undead receptionist and hurried out into the evening air. She took in a deep breath and tipped her hat. Samuel poked his head out and also took a deep breath. "Boy, now I know what they mean by getting goosebumps. What about you?"

Samuel squeaked in agreement as Gwynevere walked through the open street of the bustling city. She waved and smiled at everyone she passed. It was her nature to be a social butterfly. People like Dolly were not an uncommon sight, as they were often the creations of witches and warlocks unable to cope with the passing of their mortal lovers. Cat people, gnomes, and tiny fae folk often littered the streets with others just like Gwynevere. Samuel liked to watch all the people pass by, giving their friendly neighborly greetings.

Gwynevere hurried toward home. She wanted to get back and see if her mother had any comments about the brew she'd made earlier in the day. The lights of the streetlamps magically flickered the moment she passed beneath them.

"What do you think Mother is brewing with us, Samuel?" she asked her familiar curiously. "You don't suppose it's a youth potion? After all, Mother has been looking at herself a lot in the mirror lately."

The rat just twitched his nose and squeaked before pulling back up under her hat. "Yeah, I suppose that would almost be too obvious," she laughed.

Gwynevere passed through the gates leading out of the city toward her home, which was hidden away from the center of the city by towering oak trees. A familiar chill came upon her as the wind shifted ever so slightly. She turned to see an older, slumped woman in full witch's garb approach her. "Mama Maggie?" she gasped.

The old woman tilted her hat up and smiled with a glint in her eye. "Well now, if it isn't my dearest grandchild," she said with a chuckle. "Wandering the city alone?"

"Samuel is with me," said Gwynevere. Her noble rat poked out his head and squeaked with affirmation at the mention of his name. "What are you doing here? Mother says you don't like coming to the city."

"She would be right," said the old woman with a sigh. She revealed a lumpy bag tossed over her back. She leaned forward and adjusted her position on her walking stick. "But even I can't just conjure up fresh produce on a whim."

"Do you need my help?" Gwynevere asked with a big smile. "I don't get to see you very often. You should come back to the house."

"Your mother wouldn't allow that," the old woman scoffed. "Leave it to a Proctor to hold a vendetta. Don't worry yourself about the affairs of your elders." An odd smile appeared on the old witch's face. "I can sense great power surging through you. I assume you're planning to get into the Academy?"

Gwynevere nodded and smiled proudly. "I think I'm guaranteed," she said.

"Now that is the Merry in you," Mama Maggie chuckled. She scoffed and scuffled her shoes against the stone as she pushed up on her walking stick. "If you don't mind, dear, I need to get back. Don't be a stranger to my woods. You'll find that time has a funny way of behaving out there. Believe me when I say, your family wouldn't even know you've gone."

"Yes, ma'am," said Gwynevere with a sigh as she waved goodbye to her grandmother. The feud between Mama Maggie and her mother got in the way of her having a close relationship with such a respected and powerful member of the family. Magdalyn Proctor was a sombre witch, a title given only to those who have been dubbed masters of the magical arts. Gwynevere thought of all the exciting lessons she could learn under her tutelage. She hurried along the path toward home, skipping and singing. Her life was perfect.

Gwynevere raised her hands, and with just a hint of magical force from her palms, she pushed the giant door open. She stepped into the main hall and called out, "Mother! Father! I've returned!"

A strange silence followed. Gwynevere looked around her vacuous family manor and raised a curious brow. *How intriguing.* She breathed out and lifted her hat. Samuel ran down to her shoulder. "Huh... I wonder where they both went.... Hello?! I'm back from the Mayor's office! He was kinda scary but seemed nice and Ms. Dolly was lovely if not a little pale!"

She walked down the hall past the stairs to the kitchen. She opened the door and looked in, the brew her mother had been working on bubbled and burped. "Strange," she whispered. Her mother would never leave a brew unattended. That was witches brewing safety 101. A shadow darted across the kitchen making her jump. She spun around where she stood in the doorway, but there was nothing there.

"Hello, anyone here?!" The young witch's voice trembled ever so slightly. She grabbed the unlit oil lamp on the end table next to her and blew into it, igniting a fire. She held the lantern in front of herself, like a shield. It was always so dark in the house at night, and Gwynevere's night vision wasn't as keen as her father's. The unusual absence of both of her family members had Gwynevere on edge as she nervously flicked her fangs.

"Mother…? Father?!" Surely they wouldn't leave without a note. She scoured the bottom floor of the manor, gliding from room to room with the supernatural speed gifted to her from birth. Her eyes traversed the stairs… maybe they were just hiding in their separate rooms. She hurried up to find out. "Mommy?! Daddy?!"

The emptiness of the home began to feel foreboding and unwelcoming. Something had happened during the time she left the house and returned, and it was nothing good. The air was thick, and her vampire blood tingled at the sensation of lingering wickedness. She pushed open the door to her mother's room and gasped. All of her mother's carefully catalogued ingredient bottles had been smashed on the floor. Escaped bugs skittered from the lantern light to the dark corners of the room.

"What's going on?" Gwynevere cried out. Samuel poked his head out from beneath her hat squeaking wildly. "I know, I know, something horrible has happened." Every way she turned, another disaster. "Her books!" Gwynevere exclaimed, brushing away potion bottles that had been poured onto them, effectively destroying them. *Who would do this? Why?*

She hurried down the hall to her father's room, pushed open the door and let out a terrified scream. "Mom!!!" she cried out. Her fingers dug into the frame of the door, and then she felt herself falling and falling.

Gwynevere awoke to a cool touch on her cheek and a gentle whisper. Her eyes fluttered open to see Dolly looking down at her. "Oh dear, thank the ashes you're okay," she said with a worried smile.

"Is my mom… is she…?"

Dolly helped Gwynevere sit up. Her mom lay in the middle of her father's room. Her eyes empty, her face blue green from suffocation, she had been poisoned.

"Mom!" Gwynevere cried out, she fought the urge to vomit. Dolly wrapped her arms around her, rocking her gently back and forth, "I'm so sorry. I'm so sorry." Gwynevere clung to the ragged dress of the ghoul and sobbed.

Gwynevere became aware of other voices in the room. One distinct growling voice stood out from the others, Mayor Wimbly. He was surrounded by several officers from the elite investigative team. "Eyes peeled for any trace of Adonis Merry's whereabouts. I want every man, wolf, and pixie on this case. This is a murder and we're missing our key suspect."

An officer shook his head as he approached the Mayor, whose face immediately turned sour. "We can't find any trace of the poison used," stated one of the officers. He glanced surreptitiously over his shoulder toward Gwynevere and then whispered to the Mayor, "Whatever they forced her to swallow, it didn't leave a scent or trace to pick up."

"Impossible!" growled the Mayor. "Figure it out!"

The officer nodded, took a step backward and bolted out of the room.

Gwynevere shook her head in disbelief. "Why is he blaming this on my father...?" she whispered hoarsely. She felt Samuel crawl up her leg and onto her chest, his eyes looking wild with worry. "Oh Samuel."

Seeing that Gwynevere was awake and lucid, the Mayor approached, he filled his lungs with air and let out a weighty sigh. "Gwynevere," he spoke softly, uncomfortably so. "Your father literally confessed to the crime in the letter that you delivered to me." He thought for a moment and then continued. "As you must have known, your father had been *most* unhappy." He watched Gwynevere closely as he spoke.

Yes, thought Gwynevere. Her mother and father fought…a lot, but she knew in her heart that they *still* loved each other. With Dolly's help, she rose shakily to her feet, holding Samuel in her hand. "Sir," she addressed the Mayor with tears in her eyes. "May I see the letter?"

The Mayor considered her request and sighed. "Alright, I don't see any harm in allowing you to read it." He slipped his hand into his vest and removed a crumbled letter. He cleared his throat as Gwynevere spread the paper out so she could read it. "I apologize for the condition of the letter. I thought it was another one of your father's blusterings meant to do nothing but waste my time." He coughed into his hand and looked at Dolly.

Gwynevere disregarded the Mayor's rude statement, only slightly aware of the rivalry he and her father shared. It was by natural instinct they distrusted one another. Adonis Merry was many things. Among them, he was articulate. The letter Gwynevere held in her hand confused her—it was written in her father's handwriting, but it was not her father's words.

I confess that it was my fault, and I should suffer the blame..., Gwynevere read, her bright ruby eyes scanning the page intensely, her hands trembling. *I can only hope that my judgment comes as mercilessly as the judgment I've handed to others... Adonis Marcus Merry.*

She breathed out slowly and looked up at the Mayor. "My father did have a habit of wasting your time," she said as she took the letter and handed it to Samuel.

"Hand me the letter, Ms. Merry," said the Mayor, holding his hand out to her. "It will be needed as evidence when we find and prosecute your father."

Samuel squeaked and then leapt from Gwynevere's hand scurrying down the hall, carrying the letter in his tiny jaws. Dolly gasped as the Mayor growled and shouted at the officers controlling the crime scene. "Don't just stand there! After that darn rodent!" he shouted. "It has our only key evidence against this murderer!"

The officers piled up in the doorway and raced down the hall to find Samuel. Gwynevere stood there, mouth hanging open, stunned and unsure as to why her familiar just did what he did. The Mayor turned to her and scoffed. "This is why you can never trust a vampire," he bolted across the room to assist his men, "not even a half-blood."

Gwynevere looked down. "I'm sorry Dolly, I never expected…."

The ghoul shook her head. "No, I am," she said. "If there is anything else you need to do in this house, I suggest you do so now. The Mayor wants to close off everyone from the crime scene."

Gwynevere nodded and thanked her quietly. She took one last look at her mother's body. She turned and held her mouth, overcome with emotion. She clumsily stumbled down the stairs, following the voices of the men chasing Samuel. Thoughts like clouds streamed through her consciousness moving too quickly for her to concentrate on any single one. Samuel slipped through an egg-sized hole in the bottom of the front door, and into the night, a phalanx of officers at his furry heels.

Gwynevere slid to a stop in the kitchen. Part of her wanted to race outside and find Samuel before he got hurt. Another part of her told her to stay, that the wise old rodent knew what he was doing. Much to her relief the kitchen seemed untouched. The two officers that were taking samples of the brew she and her mother had created together had joined the other officers pursuing Samuel, who had nothing in mind but to escape and devour the evidence.

Like a moth to a flame, she slowly approached the ominous brew and peered into the massive cauldron. The radiant liquid inside bubbled and boiled, but the outside of the pot was cool to the touch.

She could hear her mother's voice, *The more active the brew, the stronger the potency*. Gwynevere wiped the tears from her eyes with her sleeve. Her mother had made this brew for a reason, and before she could talk herself out of it, she grabbed the ladle lying next to the cauldron and dipped it into the brew. She pursed her lips and slowly brought it to her mouth, sipping on it lightly with a resounding gulp.

Gwynevere released a quick breath, the world started spinning and then everything went black.

4 – Shadow

Gwynevere blinked her eyes trying to acclimate herself in the dimly lit room. She was laying on her back, staring at a barren ceiling with wooden rafters. She could hear the sound of water running.

Where am I? She pulled herself up to a sitting position. She was wedged between a wall and a shoddy bed. The room was sparse and aged, the walls stained. Cheap pottery sat atop a circular table that by some act of God was still standing. Several boxes were pushed into a corner, and at the back of the room, a window—framed by two dirty curtains—let in just enough light to see that the day had turned to dusk.

Gwynevere slowly pulled herself to her feet, brushed the dust off her clothes and readjusted her hat. She blinked and tilted her head. A furry black feline stared back at her.

"H-hello?" Gwynevere whispered. She heard the water valve shut off and a female voice humming happily to herself. She looked back at the cat in distress. "I'm terribly sorry for the intrusion," she whispered. "I have no idea how I got here. Can you tell me where I am?"

The cat meowed quietly, surprised at the new guest in his home. "Oh? I'm not sure I understand," said Gwynevere. "Are you not a familiar?"

The cat meowed at Gwynevere and leapt onto the windowsill. Gwynevere understood that was her cue to hide. She dropped down to the floor and slowly skulked under the rickety old bed. She held one hand firmly on her hat and the other against her mouth to mask her breathing. A pair of stocking feet walked out from behind the curtain. The sound of a girl's voice could be heard scoffing as she approached the windowsill. She stood mere inches from where Gwynevere hid under her bed.

"Oh, Rufus. Ever the vigilante watchdog," she said with a sigh. The cat meowed and stretched indignantly, annoyed by her remark. Gwynevere witnessed the exchange with a surprised and confused look on her face. "Right, right, watch *cat*, my utmost apologies."

She watched the girl's feet walk around the bed and slip on some worn black shoes before heading across the room to the stairs. The cat landed softly on the floor and gave her a look that demanded she stay put. The terrified young witch knew it was in her best interest to listen to the cat. She nodded and then watched as it followed the girl downstairs. Another, deeper voice could faintly be heard talking, and then the sound of the front door shutting.

"By Grimlock's beard... Mother, what have I stumbled upon?" she whispered quietly to herself. She slowly crawled out from under the bed, mumbling to herself. "I certainly cannot stay in a stranger's home. The Mayor wouldn't hesitate to call it breaking and entering. Wouldn't you say so, Samuel?"

She had for a moment forgotten that her beloved rat had run off, distracting the Ashen officials while Gwynevere made this discovery. That realization hit her hard, she rubbed her eyes, fighting back tears. She knew she had to stay strong. It was what her mother would have told her to do in this situation. Her father too. Gwynevere still couldn't comprehend the accusations that were being placed against him. There was something about the Mayor she inherently distrusted. Her father always felt the same. Too many things just didn't add up.

Cautiously, she approached the stairs, stopping for a moment to look at the drawn-back curtain, spotting the recently used old water basin and water pump, as well as the murky looking old mirror. *These poor people live in poverty,* was the first thing Gwynevere thought. She quietly took a step onto the stairs, only to freeze when she heard a man talking to himself.

"Oh Adelaide, if only you could see how much our little girl has grown to be like you," came the voice of a weary-sounding older man.

Gwynevere raised a brow curiously. She climbed up the stairs, not wanting to be seen by whoever remained in the home. She tiptoed across the room toward the single window in the upstairs living space, careful not to make any sort of noise that would alarm whoever it was downstairs. She reached the windowsill, twirled her finger and wriggled her nose. The hatched lock came undone, and the window swung partially open.

Gwynevere took in a heavy breath. The air smelled unusual to her, something about it teased at the back of her mind. Familiar, like a batch of flowers, but nothing incredibly distinguishable. She wriggled her nose again, hoisted herself onto the windowsill and then leapt out. She floated up into the air like a feather.

From her vantage point as she floated just beneath the canopy of the giant oaks, she could see very little in the way of civilization. A single road stretched out before her through the countryside. Lamps were being lit by two men, holding a lit candle attached to a stick. *Strange*, she thought. *Why don't they simply cast a fire spell to light the wick?*

The town, visible in the distance, looked small and rural, the exact opposite of everything

Gwynevere knew Ashen to be. It was only then that she realized she was no longer home. In fact, she had no idea where she was. She managed to stay aloft for some time as she aimed toward the nearby tree. She thought it best not to be seen until she had an understanding of the locals inhabiting this strange place.

Gwynevere started to teeter back and forth in the air. Her ability to levitate started to wane. She was still young, and her grasp on magic was novice at best. She attempted to grab hold of a branch before plummeting downward into a thick leafy bush. Her hat flew off her head and floated back upward in the updraft. She groaned and rubbed her head. Her hat danced in the wind, caught up in the branches of the tree.

"Rats," she muttered to herself and grunted in frustration.

The wind was filled with the strong scent of vegetation. It hit her nose with an almost pungent smell that seemed familiar yet indiscernible. She held out her hands in an attempt to bring her hat down, only to hear a low, angry meow of the familiar cat from before. Gwynevere quickly dove out of sight once more into the brush, heeding the cat's warning. She spotted him standing with his fur on end. He seemed panicked to stop her.

"Rufus? What do you see?" the girl that followed him asked. He arched his back, a growl rumbled in the back of his throat. "What is it?" The girl's voice trembled. Gwynevere slowly stepped back only to put her weight onto a dry twig. This startled the girl. She scooped up her cat and ran toward her home.

Gwynevere cocked her eyebrow, "Rufus? What a silly name for a cat." She rubbed her head, removed a twig from her tangled hair and sighed. She held out her hands and summoned her hat from the tree, brushing the leaves out of it before placing it back on her head. "Well Mother, this is a fine mess you've gotten me into." Her voice broke in the stillness of the night. "I wish you were here with me right now."

"Excuse me?" came a man's voice from the road just beyond the brush. "Who's lurking about here?"

Gwynevere gasped. She scrambled, twisting and turning in the branches, trying to figure out which way to turn, to escape.

Someone thrust a handheld lamplight through the branches of the bush where she hid. There was a flash of light, and then her head began spinning. She felt sick and dizzy, the person was saying something to her but none of it made sense. Her vision began to fade, and her head lolled from side to side, and then she blacked out.

There was a heavy knocking on the tailor's door. Thomas sighed and pushed back from his workbench, annoyed by the interruption. He was finally making progress on his first pair of shoes. He walked over to the door, mumbling to himself before turning the knob. "We're closed for the night," said Thomas as he cracked open the door and peered out.

"Thomas Moody, is your daughter about?" spoke the man outside, holding up his hand lamp.

"Inspector Morgan? Yes, yes, she is home. Why do you ask?"

"Because the last time our roads were hit with bright flashes of light, I know that she was involved in it somehow," said the man.

"That was never proven, Inspector," said Mr. Moody. "And I do not appreciate you coming by and harassing me once again on this matter."

"The people of Yorkshire are already scared of you and your daughter, Mr. Moody," said the inspector. "There are whispers about you harboring a witch within your abode."

Thomas's face turned dark at the accusation. "Are you accusing my daughter of being a witch?"

The inspector gave him a knowing look. "Why else do you think you've been receiving less business than usual? No one wants to be associated with you. Consider me a *friend* in this matter as I only wish to contain the peace."

"Please, talk lower, or else she may hear you," Mr. Moody insisted. He stole a glance at the darkened stairwell.

Evelyn heard her father's conversation with the inspector downstairs turn to inaudible whispers as she sulked on her rickety bed. She sighed and looked at Rufus who looked back at her and meowed, placing his paw on her quivering hand. "Perhaps you're right," she nodded. Her fingers nervously fiddled with the strings of her spice sacks. "I suppose there is no point in trying to make that potion tonight, Rufus," she whispered to him. She balled the sacks up and stuffed them within the torn seam of her mattress.

After a few minutes, she heard her father climbing up the stairs. He stopped and looked at her face, a mixture of exhaustion and worry.

"I didn't do anything, Father," Evelyn insisted. "I promised I wouldn't."

"I believe you," he sighed. "But the inspector is suspicious about something. That, or he's seeing ghosts."

Evelyn raised a brow at the word 'ghost.' He crossed the room to the window. He paused and studied the hatch. "Why did you unlock this?" he asked.

"What?" Evelyn looked at him confused. Rufus meowed and crawled up into her lap. "I have no reason to mess with the locks at all. Ever."

Her father peered out the window and looked around the room curiously. The night was young, but visibility was low. He eyed the scuff marks on the windowsill from what looked like the bottom of a shoe. He rubbed over it and felt some of the dry dirt between his fingers and twitched his moustache in suspicion.

"Father? Is something wrong?" asked Evelyn. She hugged Rufus tightly to her chest.

Thomas Moody was a simple man. He wasn't interested in dealing with things beyond his means of understanding. He rubbed his face and turned toward his daughter. He knew when she was lying to him, and there was nothing but sincerity in her eyes. He closed the window and twisted the lock. "No, no, I suppose there isn't," he said with a sigh. He smiled and rubbed her head gently. "I suppose I forgot to lock the hatch and the wind simply alerted me to my mistake."

Evelyn's eyes followed him as he walked toward the stairs. She too knew when he was lying, and he was doing so now, for what reason she couldn't possibly imagine. "I promised you I wouldn't do anything to upset the village or the inspector, and I won't," she said.

Her father chuckled and looked back at her. "Let them get upset," he said. "Just don't let me catch you doing anything reckless." With that, he took the stairs back to his workshop.

Evelyn knew if she asked where he was going, he would say he was just going to go close up shop, but they both knew better than that. Her father was a diligent workaholic, always struggling to make ends meet, yet somehow always finding a way to make her life without wanting. She appreciated his hard work and loved him dearly. That was why she went behind his back to purchase spices from Miss Bigsby. It was almost his birthday. His fortieth birthday, and she wanted to do something special for him.

She laid back on the rickety bed, stared at the ceiling and sighed. "Best wait until he's asleep to brew, Rufus." The cat curled up in a comfortable spot right next to her where she could easily stroke his fur. He let out a soft meow and started purring at her gentle touch. "Oh, you'll see. Father has been lonely for so long. A simple love potion and a night off would do him some good."

Rufus perked up at the words, *love potion*. He twitched his ears and meowed. "I was thinking about Miss Bigsby, Rufus," Evelyn explained. "I know she's been single just as long as Father has and she's very nice. Why, do you not think it will work?"

Rufus meowed again and rolled onto his back, stretching out his legs for more belly rubs. "Huh, shows what you know," said Evelyn as she scratched his belly. "I think that would make Father very happy."

Rufus was already asleep by the time she finished talking and purring softly with every stroke. Evelyn looked at him and sighed. Tomorrow was going to be a full moon and perhaps it would be best to wait until then. Her secret gift was always the most potent on those nights. She closed her eyes and smiled, thinking about the prospects of a better future for her father before eventually drifting off to sleep.

5 – Conflux

Gwynevere's eyes slowly focused on her surroundings. She was in the field behind her home. *How did I get here?* She sat up and rubbed her head, a low groan escaped her lips. "Oh… my head," she grumbled. Dawn was breaking through the gnarled deadwood behind her family home.

Oddly, she had somehow been transported outside the brewing shack where she had—less than a day before—slaved for hours on the special brew. But to where, she did not know. Her heart jumped in her chest at the sound of a tiny squeak approaching. The grass split through the field as Samuel made his way to her, jumping up onto her leg and crawling all the way up to greet his master.

"Samuel! You little looney bugger!" Gwynevere exclaimed. She gently scooped him up into her hands and nuzzled him against her face. "Don't you ever do anything that wild again, do you understand? I was so scared."

Samuel squeaked several times at Gwynevere in a panic. She paused and listened intently to him with her eyes widening. "The Mayor put out a warrant for both of our arrests?" she whispered loudly. "What, is he mad?"

The familiar continued chirping away, relaying more information. "He thinks I helped my father escape...?" Gwynevere's mind raced as the realization struck her. She didn't have anywhere to turn. If the Mayor put out a warrant for her, all of the local law enforcement would be searching for her. Unfortunately, most of them were werewolves, which were excellent trackers. They would have little to no problem finding her. She knew what she had to do. "Samuel," she cried, "the potion!"

The rat squeaked and Gwynevere nodded, relieved to know that her family home was currently unoccupied. She ran to the house and snuck in through the kitchen. Her jaw dropped when she spotted the cauldron tipped over on its side and all of the contents spilled onto the floor and dissolved into dust. "No! No! No!" she ran to the cauldron and dropped to her knees. She rubbed her hands over the dusty stains of the last remaining work of her mother. "It's all gone...," she whispered.

For a moment, Gwynevere felt utterly defeated. Tears filled her eyes. There had to be another way. The last thing she wanted to do was give up and be charged for a crime that she did not commit. Samuel called out to her from the top shelf of her mother's cabinet. "Curious of curiosities, what have you got there, Samuel?" She waved her hands back and forth and levitated to see what he had discovered.

"What is that? Oh!" she gasped. There on the shelf, sat a jar of familiar glowing purple liquid. "Mother's secret ingredient...?"

She pushed aside the old dusty jars full of, admittedly useless, ingredients and grabbed the glowing jar. She held the precious potion close. Samuel squeaked loudly, and then as if shouting *Geronimo*, leapt from the shelf onto her shoulder. "Come, we have to make another batch of that brew." She floated to the floor and hurried off to the brewing shack.

She threw the door open and closed it behind her. The interior of the brewing hut was a catastrophe. Jars and bottles had been upended, and all of her notes and brewing books had been seized. "You've got to be kidding me!" She sat the mystery jar down along with Samuel. Fortunately, whoever looted the hut, had left some of the necessary ingredients unscathed.

"Okay, Samuel, we've only got enough ingredients to try this once, that means we can't make any mistakes."

Samuel squeaked only once offering a suggestion. Gwynevere sighed, "It's a wonderful idea, but I don't think we have the time to go to Mama Maggie's. And as much as I'd like to be the sombre witch of Ashen right now, I'm not, so we have to make do with what we have."

Samuel did not question anymore and busied himself dashing back and forth from the shelf to the table, bringing Gwynevere everything she needed to start, from her mortar and pestle to the individual jars of ingredients.

Gwynevere helped when she could as she muttered to herself everything she could remember over and over again to try to get a clear remembrance of what she had done before. Her mother said it was perfect. It had to be perfect again, and she only had one chance to get it right.

She started with the water and salt mixture which she brought to a slow boil. She followed this by adding a mix of common spices and the key ingredient of pixie dust—which keeps components from ever settling in the mixture. The brew needed at least three hours of constant stirring with the occasional magical blessing to keep the components as fresh as when they were first placed in the water. The tail of a purple newt. Only one left in the jar. A drop of blood from a virgin—she winced as she bit her finger with her fang, puncturing the skin and managing to squeeze a few small drops into the cauldron. Finally, the dash of rat whiskers of which there was just enough left from the previous weed.

The day was growing old, the sun started to descend over the trees once more as Gwynevere worked tirelessly. The cauldron was now prepared and all she had left to do was combine it with her mother's mixture. She took hold of the glowing jar and sighed, smiling halfheartedly at Samuel. "Do you think Mother would be proud of us right now?" she asked. The little rat squeaked back at her rather aggressively. Gwynevere nodded. "Yeah, you're right. She would have hated hearing me doubt myself like that."

Samuel nodded. "You're so wise." He perked up, ready for more attention, when Gwynevere heard voices approaching. She froze in place, sharpening her half-blood vampiric hearing to pick up whatever it was that was going on. "The smell is coming from this shack, sir. Uh huh…. Yes, we already took everything of importance. Could be nothing."

It was one of the Mayor's men. Gwynevere could tell because he was speaking through half-formed teeth and speaking through a long-distance communicator. She should have known that her work was going to create a scent for werewolves to pick up. She hurried and dumped the contents of the jar into the cauldron. The flames shot up and changed colors just as a proper mix was supposed to do. "We did it, Samuel!" she squeaked.

The doorknob to the shack started to jiggle. The officer growled in agitation, realizing the door was locked. He used his strength to rip it open just as a blinding flash hit his yellow eyes. He howled, covering his hairy, human face. He sniffed the air as the fumes overwhelmed his senses and his eyes watered from the intensity of the flash. He stood in the doorway listening and protecting his face in case there was another attack. Finally, regaining his courage, he growled and poked his head into the shack. It was empty. The snarl wiped away from his face as the small orb attached to the badge on his cloak glowed.

"Well? Did you find anything?" It was Mayor Wimbly's voice. "Was it the girl?!"

The officer stood there, dumbfounded as he tried to wrap his head around what just happened. "I…I'll have to get back to you on that, sir."

Gwynevere watched as the scene was pulled away from her. She felt herself being stretched and pulled through a wormhole. Her body radiated with a brilliant aura. The shack grew smaller and smaller until it looked like a miniature toy and then disappeared. She looked around in awe at the world around her shifting, churning and molding like it was made of putty. Then she was falling and falling.

She landed with a thud into the brush where she once was, outside the mysterious home of the girl and her cat. She stood up and shook her head as she adjusted her hat and made sure Samuel was safe. He squeaked back at her. She immediately recognized the spot where she was almost discovered the night before, only a few feet away.

Gwynevere realized something in that moment she hadn't before. She wasn't teleported anywhere. The potion did not magically move her to another location. She remained exactly where she was, but the world around her had changed. It was most notable by that indiscernibly pungent floral smell coming from such an agriculturally rich countryside that certainly wasn't anywhere near Ashen.

"Samuel," she muttered as she looked around at the strangely yet familiar place, the daylight making it much more visibly different from her home. "I'm starting to think we're not in Ashen anymore." The rat squeaked excitedly. "What? No! This is very concerning! Where could this have possibly led us?"

"Uhm, excuse me," came a voice from behind Gwynevere. She jumped and grabbed hold of her hat, pulling it partially over her head as Samuel retreated. She turned to stare at the face of the young girl and her cat whom she'd stumbled across once before. Evelyn held Rufus in her arms. He licked his lips at the sight of Samuel. "Were you just talking to a... rat?"

Gwynevere was quick to react with a most unconvincing lie. "What?! No! Why would you say that? I think we all know that rats can't speak."

The two girls' eyes locked. Evelyn narrowed hers and tilted her head, taking in the pale, ruby-eyed, white-haired teen dressed in strange clothing, topped off with a silly pointy hat.

Gwynevere could tell it was hopeless. Her cover was blown. She let out a sigh and looked around. "Listen, I need your help," she pleaded. "People are after me for something I did not do, and I am desperately lost. I'll explain as much as I can if you'd please just help me find a place to hide."

While Evelyn considered the strange teen's request, Rufus chimed in, letting out a knowing meow. "What…? You really think that'd be a good idea?" she asked the cat. Rufus let out a kitty-sized grunt as Evelyn nodded. "If Father finds out about this, I'm blaming you."

Gwynevere watched excitedly as the human girl spoke to her cat just as plainly as she spoke to Samuel. "And you think it is weird I talk to *my* familiar?" she asked.

"Family-what?" Evelyn responded. "What do you mean—" She was interrupted by her father's voice, calling out to her from the shop.

"Evelyn, sweetie, I'm closing the shop for an hour to pick up a few things from town. Can I trust you not to go too far? Where are you? Evelyn? What are you doing out there?"

Gwynevere launched herself headfirst into a bush. "Yes, Father! I was just running after Rufus!" She held him up in the air. Rufus meowed, unamused. "I think he saw a rabbit or a rat or something. I'm coming in so I can lock up after you until you return!"

Her father nodded and then waved to her. He stooped by the door, hoisted a leather bag over his shoulder and followed the cobblestone path toward town.

Evelyn released a sigh of relief. "You can come out now." Evelyn and Rufus both shook their heads as Gwynevere dislodged herself from the bush and straightened her hat. "You can come with us," she motioned for the half-vampire to follow her, "but you've got to do something about that silly hat."

Gwynevere watched her with an insulted look on her face. But right now, she needed all the help she could get. With a huff, she pulled her hat from her head and pushed the point down, so it didn't make her stand out. She held it close to her chest and followed Evelyn with Samuel nestled on her shoulder, blending into her silver hair.

Evelyn held the door open and beckoned Gwynevere inside. She snuck a peek out the door, hoping that her father nor anyone else noticed her odd guest. Once the strange girl was inside, Evelyn closed the door and gasped.

"What did you mean when you called Rufus a familiar?" she asked hastily.

Gwynevere jumped. "Hey, easy!" She popped her hat back up and plopped it on her head. "What do you mean by what do I mean? You *are* a witch, aren't you?"

"A witch?!" Evelyn gasped as she pushed her finger to her lips in a panic. "You're not supposed to use words like that around here!"

"What? What else would you call it?" Gwynevere asked. She wrinkled her nose in confusion and flicked her sharp fangs nervously.

Evelyn looked at her for several long seconds and then grabbed her by the shoulders. Gwynevere jumped back and hissed at the girl. "If you want my help, you'll follow me." Evelyn all but pushed her up the stairs to the living space where she lived with her father. "Stay here!"

Evelyn scurried off into the bathing room and returned with an old mirror. "Here," she nearly shoved it into Gwynevere's face. The half-vampire reeled back in surprise as the two girls both looked at her reflection. "I don't understand...," Evelyn whispered.

"I'm a dhampir, or a half-vampire," said Gwynevere. "It means I don't have any of those negative traits associated with being fully undead. For instance, I don't want to suck your blood."

Evelyn gave her a strange look. Gwynevere wondered if she felt insulted.

"Listen, don't take it personally, I'm sure your blood is quite tasty, I simply don't need it or crave it. Didn't you notice I was standing outside in the sunlight just fine?"

"Well… actually, that is somewhat of a relief," said Evelyn. "But vampires are not supposed to be real. I mean… they're just old folklore meant to scare children… or be romanticized by Polidori in arguably the greatest book ever written…."

Gwynevere eyed the mostly barren room, curious where any books could be stored. "You know, you're kind of odd yourself," she said as they both caught Samuel and Rufus staring each other down. "Oh, would you stop looking at him like that? He's not food."

Rufus meowed as if to say, *Are you sure?* Evelyn raised a brow and looked at Gwynevere. "You were in my house yesterday evening?" It was more of an accusation than a question.

Gwynevere sighed and nodded. "Yes but let me explain." She noticed the young girl's eyes begin to glow and several objects in the room were now floating in the air. "Are you sure the word *witch* isn't an accurate observation?"

"You desecrated the privacy of my living space?! When I was most immodest?!"

"Well… I didn't choose where I showed up, it just sort of happened and—"

Evelyn breathed out in a burst. Using her magic, she sent several pieces of her father's tailoring equipment, rocketing at Gwynevere.

Gwynevere's eyes glowed back, stopping the objects in midair, she smiled and sent the objects back to their rightful place. Evelyn stumbled backward in surprise. "As my mother would say, you're powerful Evelyn, but ever so erratic."

"I never had a mother to teach me these things," Evelyn muttered. She looked at Gwynevere, unsure what to do. "Who are you and why are you here?"

"My name is Gwynevere Merry," she explained. "I am from Ashen, a city where people that look like me are as common as the grass is green. *Witch* is just another term for any woman who can cast magic. It's something you're proud of and *no one* will judge you for it."

"Well, my name is Evelyn Moody. I've lived here in Yorkshire all my life. My father's a tailor and we do not speak of magic. I once lit a tree on fire trying to help the townsmen light the streetlamps, and now my father has to deal with a police inspector who won't leave me alone."

"Don't speak of magic? That sounds awful," said Gwynevere. She gestured toward Evelyn's cat. "Yet no one questions your familiar?"

"Rufus has been in the family since I was born," said Evelyn. "Sixteen years."

"Don't you think that's a little old for a typical cat?" asked Gwynevere.

"Well, he likes a good steak," said Evelyn. "When we can afford it."

Rufus meowed in confirmation that this was true. Gwynevere looked at him as she slowly came to another realization. "So... this means... the potion brought me to another world... one without magic... or anything like home. Is this... this is the human realm?!"

"What do you mean the human realm?" asked Evelyn.

"When I was a little girl, my mother told me that there was a place called the human world that was completely forbidden. It sounded like a really terrifying place to visit. People from Ashen are forbidden to go to this realm. I didn't actually think it was real."

Evelyn tilted her head curiously. "That sounds... weird," she admitted. "And yet you're here. How?"

"A potion," Gwynevere explained. "Something my mother and I made. Well... I made... she just added a special ingredient. I drank it and then poof, here I am... strangely in your bedroom."

"You made a conflux potion," said Evelyn.

"A what?" asked Gwynevere, now it was her turn to be confused.

"A conflux potion!" said Evelyn excitedly. "What you just said! It makes sense!"

"What are you talking about?" asked Gwynevere. She watched curiously as Evelyn ran across the room and jumped onto her bed. "Are humans always this excitable?"

Evelyn ignored her. She rolled across the bed and waved her hands. The bed slid across the floor. She dropped down and pulled out a secret compartment from her mattress. "I usually hide things in my mattress when I don't want my father to know about something," she explained. "He helped me make this little hovel to hide a bunch of other things he doesn't want people like the inspector to find."

"That hole? Has it always been there?" asked Gwynevere curiously. "It looks big enough that you could fit in."

Evelyn shrugged. "Not sure how far back it goes, but it's proved useful for the little things that mattered."

Evelyn proceeded to pull out several books that were stashed away. She set down *The Vampyre* by John Polidori among many other occult stories. She then pulled out an old, leather-bound book that was closed with a lock and key and set it down in front of Gwynevere. Samuel squeaked and sniffed the air. He ran down Gwynevere's shoulders and onto the floor, focusing his attention on the book and behaving erratically.

"W-what is that?" asked Gwynevere.

"It's a book my dad gave me when I turned thirteen," Evelyn explained. She grabbed it up in her arms, hopped on her bed, and welcomed Gwynevere to sit next to her. The sight of Samuel on the floor was too much for Rufus. He leapt to the floor and chased the rat who darted around the room at lightning speed before running up the wall and climbing onto the old rafters in the ceiling.

Gwynevere laughed as Rufus let out a disappointed gurgle. "You'll have to try a bit harder than that, I'm afraid."

"They seem like they'll get along just fine, yes?" joked Evelyn. She waved her hand, the lock popped off the book and it opened. "There never was a key." Gwynevere sat beside her watching her intently.

"This book," Gwynevere stated. "It looks oddly familiar. Like my mother's old recipe book."

Evelyn looked at her and made a curious face. "It is my mother's old recipe book," she explained. She began turning the pages and rubbing her hand over the handwritten words, etched into the parchment of the book.

It was a handwriting that Gwynevere found all too familiar. It was the same as the handwriting she had stared at a thousand times over. Samuel started squeaking excitedly, he too noticed the familiarity of the book even before his master. Evelyn flipped through it, skimming each page. Gwynevere slowly became more and more aware of what was going on.

"Here it is," said Evelyn. She pointed to one of the pages in the back of the book marked as an advanced brew. "Conflux potions. Usually require two people to make them because the active ingredients of elder witch blood, white sage, apple vinegar, and ground earthworms make this a very volatile mixture. It's often paired with an individually brewed solution meant to protect the brewer when mixed. Drinking a conflux potion peels away the fabric of reality and allows its brewer to see things that were never meant to be found."

Gwynevere trembled, listening to Evelyn speak. Her eyes started to water as she reached out and touched the etchings. Evelyn looked at her, confused to say the least. "Never meant to be found, you say...?" she whispered. "Mother?"

"Uhm, are you okay?" Evelyn asked. She looked at Gwynevere's eyes. "Are you crying?"

"My mother is dead," whispered Gwynevere.

The sudden news took her aback. She wanted to tell her how sorry she was for her loss, but there was a strange intensity in Gwynevere's reaction.

"I helped my mother make this potion," Gwynevere continued, "because she wanted me to learn something very important about our family history."

"I-I am sorry," Evelyn muttered. "I'm not… sure I understand…."

"She was murdered by somebody close to her before she could tell me," said Gwynevere. "I took the potion to find out for myself and it brought me here. Now I see you carry around a book of your own, claiming it to be your mother's."

"But… my mother…?" Evelyn started. Rufus raised his tail in alarm. His whiskers twitched and he meowed loudly to interrupt the girls. "What is it, Rufus?" He jumped onto the windowsill and looked out, directing Evelyn to do the same. "Oh no!" Her father was returning to the shop earlier than expected, the police inspector leading him. "Gwynevere, you need to hide."

"Hide?" Gwynevere looked around and rubbed her eyes. "There really is nowhere to hide. I could cast a spell and become a shadow, but it would only last a short while."

"You can…?!" Evelyn exclaimed.

"It's just a simple spell that has to be cast with a verbal execution," said Gwynevere.

"No way!" Evelyn exclaimed.

Gwynevere looked at her and shrugged. "Yeah way? Oh, I forgot, you don't just know about these kinds of things," she said as she stood. She raised her hands toward Samuel. The rat familiar jumped from the wooden ceiling beam into her arms. Gwynevere twitched her nose. "Spectro umbra."

Instantly, she turned into a faceless, bodiless silhouette against the wall. Evelyn raised her brows in awe. Gwynevere moved toward the bed, becoming one with its shadow on the floor. "If I stay still, no one will notice me."

Evelyn nodded. "Oh wait!" She realized the bed was still pulled out and the books spread out on the floor. "Hold on!"

She waved her hand as the books flew back into the small hole and the secret compartment closed. She could hear the door downstairs open just about the time the bed moved back into place. "Evelyn?" called her father. "Evelyn, is that you?"

"Y-yes, Father!" Evelyn called out. "I was just, uhm, cleaning!"

Evelyn waved her hands and summoned a broom that was tucked away in the cluttered corner of the room. Her father rushed up the stairs to find Evelyn, broom in hand, smiling back at him. Rufus stretched slowly and let out an exaggerated yawn from the windowsill.

Gwynevere studied the older gentleman from the shadow of the bed. She wondered how much he knew about her mother, given the implications. She desperately wanted to talk to him, but she knew she would have to wait—another set of footsteps pounded up the stairs.

Evelyn's chipper demeanor dimmed at the sight of the inspector. He walked past her father and approached her, standing only inches from her face. "Hello there, Ms. Moody," he said unpleasantly. "Quite a day we're having, yes?"

"Inspector Morgan, was it?" she asked smiling politely. "Father? Why is he in our house?"

Thomas sighed, he looked exhausted and defeated. The inspector seemed to feed off of the man's silence. "I just issued a warrant to search your premises, that is all," he answered. "Your father is exercising his right to remain silent while I do so."

"And should I do the same?" asked Evelyn. Her heart racing with a sudden sense of fear.

Rufus growled at the inspector. The man held up his hand to him and waved. "Good kitty," he said. "Stay."

"Rufus, come here," said Evelyn. He jumped from the windowsill and rushed over to her, leaping up into her arms. The inspector moved toward her bed, and she stepped in front of him blocking his path.

The man reeled back, surprised that this girl would dare to block his path, but she stood her ground, holding Rufus in her arms. He looked toward Thomas and chuckled. He continued searching the sparsely furnished room, poking at a pile of boxes and randomly assorted junk. "You folks live day to day on the tiny pittance you receive from your tailor shop. Yet somehow, there is always something going on down this way that has the townspeople talking." He grinned a horrible, yellow-toothed smile at Evelyn.

"We have no idea what you are suggesting, Inspector."

"Oh?" he raised his eyebrows in mock surprise. "Is that so? Then what about those spices you purchased from Miss Bigsby? Hmm? She found it rather odd that you stopped by at such a random hour of the night before closing to buy...," he tapped his bottom lip with his finger. "Oh yes, mustard seeds, sage and ginger."

"W-why is that any of your business?" asked Evelyn. She locked eyes with her father who seemed distraught at such a revelation.

"It is my business because people have made it my business," said the inspector. "I originally came to Yorkshire because of all the reports of strange happenings over the last several years and I have since made it my permanent residence. That being said, it is still within my power, as well as my obligation, to report any strange findings and suspicious activities to my superiors and the church."

"He is just doing his job, sweetheart," Thomas said softly.

Evelyn looked at him and sighed. She sat on her bed, stretching her legs out over where Gwynevere hid in the shadows, protecting her. "Go ahead then," she said bitterly. "I hid the ingredients in pouches in my mattress. I was going to use them as a surprise heartwarming soup for Father's birthday. But I guess taking everything from us is not enough. Now you must also rob us of our happiness."

With a trembling finger she pointed to the seam of her mattress. The inspector, unmoved by her words, reached down and pulled at it, taking note the thread was fastened to the mattress and only came undone with some effort. He looked at Evelyn quietly, but Evelyn only looked at her father with heartbreaking sadness. It was clear he felt shame for having this happen now of all times. The inspector pulled out the spices and sniffed them. "Yet you hid them so well?" he asked.

"I did say it was for a surprise present for my father's birthday," Evelyn said. "Or do I need to explain the word *surprise* to you?"

The inspector looked at Evelyn and snarled. Gwynevere laid perfectly still. She had to focus. The spell would wear off soon. The inspector crossed the room and pulled back the curtain to the washroom. He stood for a long moment staring at the simple rusted basin. "I suppose I am wasting my time here," he said. "So sorry to bother you further, Mr. Moody, but as you know, I can never be too careful."

"I understand," said Thomas. The inspector walked past him and down the stairs with the spice bags in hand. He looked back at Evelyn and sighed. "Honey, I—"

"Don't you have some shoes to make or something?" asked Evelyn. "I mean, we are living on pennies as it is. Better make every cent count."

He looked at her and then held up his hands in surrender. It was useless to argue with Evelyn on this matter. He knew he should not have let the inspector inside their home, but he didn't know how to explain to his teenage daughter that his hands were tied in this matter. "Inspector Morgan! Please, let me see you out."

Evelyn waited until she heard them both step outside the door before looking down. "Okay, I think I got rid of him."

Gwynevere reappeared and let out a heavy sigh. "That seemed very intense." She wiped an arm across her forehead where a sheen of sweat had formed.

"Inspector Morgan is the man who keeps harassing us because of my powers," said Evelyn. "I think he knows we're lying to him and it's only getting worse as I get older."

"I wouldn't trust him," said Gwynevere. "I don't trust people like that anyways." She brushed herself off. "I don't know how long the potion is going to last on me this time. I feel we have just now only scratched the surface."

"What do we do?" asked Evelyn.

Gwynevere shrugged. "Is there a place we could talk that is safer than this?" she asked.

"Well, a lot of Yorkshire is farmland," said Evelyn. "But I guess you'd be right at home with a few scarecrows in a cornfield."

Samuel and Rufus both looked at each other, then their masters, unsure what to make of this newly formed alliance. Gwynevere looked at her and chuckled. "Honestly? I'd probably prefer it."

6 – Discovery

The sun was on the descent over the cornfields as Gwynevere followed Evelyn through the tall stalks. The two had been mostly silent since leaving the tailor's house together, each of them carrying their familiars, with Evelyn also carrying her mother's book. They reached the looming shadow of a scarecrow that overlooked the open field. Gwynevere looked up at him and grinned under the shadowy brim of her witch's hat.

"I like him," she said. "So much personality."

"I call him Mr. Crow," said Evelyn. She sat down and leaned against the wooden pole that held the hay stuffed mannequin aloft. She set Rufus down next to her and laid the large book on her lap. "I come out here sometimes when I want to think or read in silence. There was a time when Father had a lucrative business. Customers were coming and going by the minute, and there was never much time for anything else but to tend the shop."

Gwynevere nodded. She sat down with Evelyn and let Samuel sit on her lap. Rufus stared at the rat with intent as the two continued their standoff. "So, where were we...?" Evelyn asked. She flipped through the pages of the book to find the conflux potion recipe.

"We were here... talking about Mother," said Gwynevere. She tapped her finger on the book, and then something burst inside of her. Tears spilled down her cheeks and her breath became ragged. Evelyn reeled back in surprise, but Gwynevere pulled her close, sobbing into her shoulder. "I miss my mother. I don't understand how this happened. I don't want to be without her!"

"Hey, it's okay!" Evelyn said gently. She dropped the book and wrapped her arms around Gwynevere and held her tight. "It's okay! You know, I never had a mother in my life. You're lucky! No, *blessed*! You're blessed to have known her, and she sounds like she might have been the best mom ever!" Evelyn fought for the right thing to say.

Gwynevere sobbed, taking in deep breaths. She buried her face into Evelyn's neck. "Your blood... I smell it," she said softly.

Evelyn blinked. How was she supposed to respond to that? "Is that... good? Not good?" she asked.

Gwynevere pulled away slowly and wiped her tears. "I'm sorry," she said. "So much has happened so fast, I just haven't had a moment to grieve. I got overwhelmed."

"No, it's fine," Evelyn replied, trying to comfort her friend. "I just, you know, don't know if I want you biting my neck, that's all. No offense."

The clouds overhead moved quickly across the sky as the wind churned through the cornfield. Gwynevere smiled at Evelyn's words. "I don't need blood like that," she explained. "But the vampire in me gives me a sixth sense of smell. You smell just like Mother and...."

Evelyn looked at Gwynevere, her eyes trailed off to an unexplored, unfathomable place. She reached out and cupped her hand to Gwynevere's cheek and smiled. "You're thinking what I'm thinking, right?" asked Evelyn.

"I'm thinking that I know what you're thinking and I'm thinking it too," said Gwynevere with a nod.

"Your mother is my mother...," whispered Evelyn.

Gwynevere looked at Evelyn for a moment, then reached out and embraced her in the most loving embrace. "I always wanted a sister!"

"Oof!" Evelyn grunted as she was squeezed extra hard. "You've got some *strength* there."

"Sorry, the vampirism makes me a lot stronger than I look."

"I'll say." Evelyn laughed and brushed her hair from her face. She waited for a moment, bracing herself for what she knew would be a difficult question. "How did she die?" she asked. Gwynevere breathed out and closed her eyes, her body stiffened. Evelyn reeled back. "I'm sorry. You don't have to—"

"She was murdered," Gwynevere said quietly. "She was poisoned… allegedly, by my father."

"Your father?" Evelyn gasped. There was a slow build up in the wind once again. Her eyes began to glow, and she quickly looked away and rubbed them. "Sorry. When I get emotional, sometimes I can't control my magic."

Gwynevere nodded in understanding, knowing full well that Evelyn had no real training and that was to be expected. "They never got along much." She started to tear up thinking about it again. "My mother always told me that it had been an arranged marriage, that she had no say in the matter. I was the special gift that made a loveless marriage bearable. Father always had his eyes on another woman, a judge. He never said it to my face but the way he spoke of her sometimes, I could tell, you know?" She rubbed her watery eyes. "That makes it all the more hurtful that they would want to place blame on me for helping him, when I did *no* such thing."

"Who is blaming you?" asked Evelyn.

"Our city mayor," said Gwynevere. "He's a werewolf and they never got along as vampires and werewolves tend to do."

"And your father was...?" Evelyn awkwardly pointed to her mouth, hoping not to offend Gwynevere.

"A vampire? Yes," she confirmed. "You're not a vampire. Mother didn't have any of those traits."

"Oh, right," said Evelyn, shaking her head like that was a dumb question to even ask.

"My father was a judge on the Ashen Council Board," said Gwynevere. "Nobody liked him that much, but he always seemed to keep company. I remember running around the manor halls when I was a child and bumping into all sorts of crazy characters my dad made nice with in his business. He especially made nice with a powerful judge vampire woman. Though I'm not sure what he saw in her. She was nice enough, but always busy. Then there is Dolly. Oh, you would love Dolly. She is the nicest undead you would ever meet. Mother helped give her life after Mayor Wimbly had her patched back together and—"

She caught Evelyn staring at her, bewildered by what must seem outlandish to someone from the human world.

"Sorry," said Gwynevere. "I forget that what I consider ordinary, to you it's quite extraordinary."

"It sounds magical," said Evelyn. "It makes me wonder why I am here and not there. I wonder if Father knows about it."

"He might? I'm not sure," Gwynevere shrugged. She patted Samuel on his head and rubbed a finger between his ears. "I knew you were a witch as soon as I met Rufus. He's a familiar. Spiritual servants of a natural-born witch that live their whole lives in tandem with their masters," Gwynevere explained.

Evelyn looked at Rufus, petting him and smiling. "I guess that would explain a lot of things," she said. "Like how people look at me funny when we carry on a conversation."

Rufus meowed loudly, making Evelyn laugh. "Hey! It wasn't that obvious! I'm still learning."

She sighed and looked at Gwynevere. "Sometimes, when I get really angry or scared, things happen, and I lose control of what I'm doing." Rufus meowed again and she nodded. "Yes, yes, I'm telling her now in case it happens."

"What kind of *things* happen?" Gwynevere inquired.

"Earthquakes, spontaneous levitation, sometimes even thunderstorms," she explained.

"That's... actually *not* that normal," said Gwynevere. "You must have a lot of raw power from so many years without training."

"I guess so. Do you think that, I mean, now that you're here, you could help me?" asked Evelyn.

"I'm not trying to make excuses. I mean I'll try… but I don't even know half of the things that Mother knew."

"You had a chance to learn from her though," Evelyn reminded her. "That is a lot more than I ever had."

Gwynevere nodded, saddened that now, she only had memories of her mother. She'd never see her smile again, experience her touch, hear her voice. "You know, I don't know if my father killed my mother. I mean, he certainly could have, and they argued all the time." She sat quietly for a moment thinking. "There was always this sense of calmness about him. I know he loved me, and he wanted what was best… so why would he do such a thing knowing what it would do to my life?"

Evelyn shrugged. "Maybe you don't know him as well as you thought you did?" she grimaced when she realized what she'd said. But Gwynevere didn't flinch.

"I suppose you could say the same about your father," replied Gwynevere.

"That is true," Evelyn sighed. She glanced down at the potion book laying on her lap. "Hmm," she mused, "that's interesting."

"What?"

"It says here that the reactivity of the potion is based on whether or not the user is put in danger. You can return to the place of origin by reciting a simple spell. Oh, this doesn't sound good."

"What is it?" asked Gwynevere.

"You can also be banished back to your place of origin, especially in the presence of a protective ward spell or other territorial protection spell."

"I suppose that would make sense, though I never uttered a spell to return home," said Gwynevere. She sat there for several long seconds in silence, contemplating.

"You don't have to figure this out alone." She placed her hand softly on Gwynevere's shoulder. "We're in this together now. We both owe it to our mother to find out what happened to her and bring whoever is responsible to justice!"

"I agree," nodded Gwynevere. "I think we should start by talking to your father. He knew our mom... and I'm quite sure he knew there was something different about her. She never was one to hide her *abilities*," she clarified.

"Not my father," said Evelyn. "He has done everything he can to make sure I hide who I *really* am from the world. That being said," Evelyn tilted her head, "I think he is beginning to learn that he cannot control me so easily. And... to make things worse, he's become a lot more skittish because of the nosey police inspector."

"It sounds like he is hiding your *abilities* because he loves you," said Gwynevere.

"So, what you're saying is, we don't corner him and then threaten him with those fangs of yours, *if* he doesn't tell us the truth?" snickered Evelyn.

"Evelyn!" Gwynevere gasped in mock offense. She wiped away the last of her tears and playfully shoved her sister.

"I'm kidding!" laughed Evelyn. "Just trying to lighten the mood here."

Both Samuel and Rufus looked at each other and sighed. It was clear their instinctual rivalry would have to be put aside for the sake of their masters. They were going to need all the help they could get in the coming times and they will surely be lost without their trusty familiars to guide them.

7 - Moon

It was late afternoon when Thomas Moody returned to his shop. The glowing orb of the sun was barely visible above the treetops and the moon was making itself known in the sky. He couldn't afford to close his shop, but he had to trek into town and haggle with the local vendors for materials to make his shoes. Which was the only thing he was able to sell in the last few days, since customers stopped coming to his shop. He paused at the door, wondering how he would be able to face his daughter after the stint with Inspector Morgan.

He fiddled with the lock, pushed the door open and stepped inside. It was dim with the oil lamp running dry. Thomas shuffled over to the counter and slung his pack of goods on top of it, with a *thunk*. He removed his glasses and wiped off the sweat and grime of the day with his sleeve. "Evelyn, are you home?" He called out, hearing movement upstairs.

"Father? Can you please come here? I have something very important to talk to you about."

Thomas made his way up the stairs. "Yes, sweetheart?" He noticed the upstairs room was dark as well. "Are we out of oil for every lamp in the house?"

Suddenly, all of the lights came on at once, each lamp burning bright with fire. Thomas jumped, striking his shoulder on the door frame. His daughter and a mysterious, pale-faced stranger were sitting on her bed. "You tell me, Father," Evelyn replied.

"Evelyn? W-who is your friend?" his voice trembled, seeing the bright shine of red in Gwynevere's eyes.

"I was hoping you'd know that already," said Evelyn, crossing her arms. Rufus crossed the room and sat defiantly at Thomas's feet.

Thomas looked at her, then to Gwynevere with confusion. "I, uh, I don't understand."

"Sir, my mother was named Adelaide Proctor, once upon a time," said Gwynevere. Both girls watched Thomas's demeanor completely shift. She too crossed her arms and raised a brow. "Ring any bells?"

"Adelaide?" he gasped, telling the girls plenty with his reaction. His mouth fell open as his eyes twinkled with a sudden rush of memories. "That would make you—"

"Her sister," Gwynevere smiled, revealing her fangs. "We figured that out."

"No... well, yes," said Thomas as he shook his head. "You're from Ashen."

"You know about Ashen?!" cried Evelyn. "All this time we've been living here, struggling and hiding, and you knew all about this magical place where my mother was from, and you *hid* it from me?!"

"No, no we couldn't, Evelyn," he said softly. "May I?" He gestured toward the bed.

Evelyn nodded, giving him a look that said, *You're not out of the woods yet.*

He sat beside his daughter with a heavy sigh. "I can only assume there are details that your mystery sister here has yet to tell you?"

The girls looked at each other then back at him. "No?" said Gwynevere. "I've told her literally everything I know about what's going on up to this point."

Thomas looked at her and shook his head. "Then there is a lot you do not know about the world you've come from," he explained.

Gwynevere took in a deep breath. It was hard to continually explain what had happened to her, to her mother. "Listen, I came here because I had nowhere to go. My mother… our mother, was murdered and—"

"Adelaide was what?!" Thomas gasped and jumped to his feet.

"Father, listen to her for a moment," said Evelyn, grabbing his arm and pulling him down beside her.

Gwynevere breathed out and nodded. "Yes, but we're not sure why," she said. "The Mayor is blaming me and my father as being responsible. I admit… it doesn't look good for my father… but I have done nothing wrong!"

Rufus sniffed the air curiously, and then leapt onto the windowsill. Evelyn watched him quizzically. Her father stood again and rubbed his head. "Listen young lady," he said to Gwynevere. "If you are who you say you are and…," he eyed her witch's hat, "I believe you are… you really shouldn't be here."

"But where else am I to go?" asked Gwynevere. "My mother had me help her develop a potion that allowed me to slip into your world. I'm not sure why, but there had to be a reason. I can only assume she intended for Evelyn and me to meet."

"It is not simply because someone said you can't do it," said Thomas. "It is the law, and the law is there for a reason. The human world does not take kindly to things like magic and monsters."

"Monsters?!" Gwynevere gasped, offended.

"Like it or not, that is how it is," said Thomas. "The higher orders of your world banned all forms of contact with our world for that and many other reasons. You being here is putting all of us in danger."

Evelyn turned back and looked at her father. "Yet I have been here all this time, and nothing has come of it! Why is that?" she demanded.

Thomas looked at her, his hands fell heavily to his sides. "Because... your mother was the one who broke this law," he said. "When she had to return to her home back in Ashen, you and I were not permitted to follow her... believe me, I wanted to. Your mother and I were in love, and when we had you...," he looked at his daughter, his eyes filled with compassion, "you were punished with exile the moment you were born."

Rufus arched his back, a low growl gurgled in his throat, he lashed out at the window hissing.

"What is wrong, Rufus?!" Evelyn gasped.

The cat continued to growl as the full moon was completely visible through the window. That was when they heard a loud, bloodcurdling howl echo from the darkness beyond the roads outside. Gwynevere's nose twitched as she flicked her fangs nervously and stood. "We have to go!" she shouted in a loud whisper.

"What in the heavens was that?" asked Thomas, his face filled with fear.

"It's the police," she said. "They're coming to get me and take me back!"

"Police?" Evelyn hurried over to the window, where Rufus eyed a massive black shadow moving past an outdoor lantern. She picked up Rufus and hurried to her father. "Is the downstairs door locked?"

"What? No, I didn't—"

Before he could finish his sentence, Evelyn whisked past him down the stairs. Thomas attempted to stop her but Gwynevere held him back.

Evelyn quietly descended the stairs and stepped into the darkness of her father's shop. A menacing growl rattled the door from outside. The knob turned and the door slowly opened, Evelyn caught a glimpse of a mouth filled with razor-sharp teeth and a hairy snout. She threw up her hand, slamming the door shut on the surprised beast. She slid the bolt into place and then began pushing box after box of supplies and lastly, the front counter, sealing the entrance completely.

The beast snarled and scratched at the door. After a moment, the clawing stopped. Evelyn knew he hadn't given up. He was just looking for another way in. She tried to swallow the fear that grew inside of her. The lights began to flicker, and the objects scattered about the room began to float and swirl around her. She fought to bring her magic under control, she had to protect her father! The window! She spun and raced up the stairs. Gwynevere had already sealed the window with an upturned bed and was hurriedly stacking boxes behind it.

Thomas dropped to his knees in a state of shock. "This can't be happening," he cried to himself. "Adelaide, what do I do? What do I do?"

"Sir, get ahold of yourself," ordered Gwynevere, grabbing his arm and shaking him. The beast released a bloodcurdling howl and slammed into the window, making the entire house shake. Thomas covered his ears and shivered. Samuel squeaked and ran up Gwynevere's leg, up to her shoulder and hid in her hair. "Sir?! Sir?"

"What?!" he cried out. He looked at the young half-vampire with an expression of terror.

"My familiar says that there is another way out of this house," said Gwynevere. "If we stay here much longer, we're going to become werewolf food, and I don't want to be werewolf food!"

"I don't know of another entrance." He cast a quizzical glance at Evelyn, who shook her head. "Look, if you know of a way to get out of here, by all means." He grabbed Gwynevere by the shoulder. "Please, don't let anything happen to Evelyn."

Gwynevere smiled at him and nodded. "I won't let *anything* happen to her," she said with confidence.

She held out her hand to Evelyn. Rufus charged across the room and leapt into her arms. Gwynevere flung open the hidden hatch where Evelyn stored her books. Samuel leapt from her shoulder and disappeared into the hole, squeaking all the way.

"Does he seriously want us to follow him in there?" asked Evelyn. "Into the wall?"

"Are you scared of tight spaces?" asked Gwynevere. Another bang rocked the house and the window shattered.

"Not anymore!" said Evelyn. She dropped to her knees and crawled into the hole.

Thomas stole a quick glance at the window, the beast was tearing the bed to pieces. It wouldn't be long before he'd breached the makeshift barrier. Gwynevere grabbed him by the collar of his shirt. "Go!"

"Wait, what?" he gasped.

The time for hesitation was over. Using her vampire strength, she threw him to the ground, waved her hand, sending him flying across the floor into the hole.

Rufus meowed, as if to say, *Is it my turn?* Gwynevere nodded to him. "I have the gifts my father gave me," she told him. "If I do not make it, make sure they follow Samuel. He will know how to get them out of the house."

The cat nodded with respect before jumping into the small hole. Gwynevere had just sealed off the hole when the werewolf smashed through the barricade. The young witch stopped the flying debris in midair with a flick of her hand. The towering monster pulled its muscular body through the small window. She flicked her razor-sharp teeth with her tongue and sighed.

"You know, the Mayor is going through a lot of trouble to get me back." She crossed her arms and raised an eyebrow. "Do you realize the kind of damage you're causing here?! There is no way this is ordinance. I know the law because my dad's a judge."

The werewolf glared down at the ruby-eyed teen and snarled, showing his massive, fanged teeth. He was a hulking beast, nearly seven feet tall, its black fur shimmered from the moonlight streaming through the window. She would have to be careful, one well-placed slash from his claws could kill her.

"Who are you?" she demanded. "What does the Mayor think he will gain from hurting me or these people? Why would you risk yourself to such exposure?"

The werewolf sniffed the air and turned his attention to the hidden hatch in the walls. It was clear that he knew where the others went. Gwynevere had to think fast. She clapped her hands as hard as possible. "Displodo!"

An explosion of light and acrid smoke filled the room. The massive beast snarled angrily, pawing at its burning eyes and nose. It swiped a massive paw at Gwynevere, inches from her face. She dove and rolled, crashing against the wall just beneath the window. The beast slashed again batting her hat from her head. Gwynevere snatched it from the floor, and leapt out the window, landing on the lower rooftop. She quickly surveilled the tiny town, bathed in moonlight—wondering to herself if they had heard the werewolf. She ran along the rooftop praying Samuel was keeping her newfound sister and her father safe.

Evelyn and her father squeezed through the crawlspace between the walls. The tip of Evelyn's finger glowed brightly, enabling her to see Samuel as he scurried ahead of them. "Did you know the walls were hollow?" Evelyn whispered to her father.

"No," he replied softly. "This building was constructed long before I was born."

The house shook violently. The monster was tearing away at the walls. Rufus released a low murmur from deep in his throat, it was as if he was saying *Hurry, hurry!*

"Most likely this wall was built like this as an escape route. During the war, the soldiers used to attack villagers and commandeer their houses."

"Interesting," was all Evelyn could think of replying. Samuel descended down another hole, squeaking loudly and beckoning them to follow. Rufus meowed in agreement, frustrated by his view of Thomas's hindquarters. Evelyn leapt into the hole.

She was surprised she kept falling and stopped her descent just inches before she crashed to the ground. "Wait, Father," she called out, "don't jump!" She illuminated the room with her finger.

Samuel squeaked at her to hurry. "Well, you could have told me there was a ladder," Evelyn replied, fussing at the rodent. She waited for her father to climb down the ladder. Rufus climbed down a step or two and then leapt gracefully to the floor. Evelyn held out her hand. A ball of light appeared, hovering just above her palm, illuminating the room and revealing a network of tunnels. Samuel spun toward her, squeaking frantically. Evelyn nodded and followed him into the darkness. She tossed the orb of light into the air, and it hovered above them, lighting the way.

"Can you actually understand what that rat is saying?" asked Thomas.

"He's saying he can smell the exit," said Evelyn.

"Evelyn, I know I have told you to suppress your magic in the past, but if the worst comes...."

"I won't let anything happen to you, Father," said Evelyn. "I can control myself. Don't worry," she gave him a reassuring smile.

Thomas breathed out and sighed as she moved further ahead. "I was going to say save yourself and forget about me...," he whispered, unsure if she heard him or not.

Thomas was proud of his daughter. She was incredibly brave. He knew living a life of lies, hiding who she was, had been incredibly hard on her. He released a heavy sigh and followed, leaving behind the sound of the terrifying monster, tearing apart his home, his life.

8 - Spice

Gwynevere remained hidden in the tall rows of corn. She knew the night-stalking beast was close. She cautiously worked her way through the field, guided by the light of the full moon. There it was—the scarecrow.

The dry crackling sound of cornstalks rubbing against one another was growing louder. The werewolf was near. She wrapped her fingers around the wooden pole that held the scarecrow up and whispered, "Spectro umbra."

Gwynevere vanished. One moment she was there, the next she wasn't. The werewolf bounded over to where she had been standing. The creature raised its snout to the sky—Gwynevere's scent still hung in the air. Confused, the great beast began to spin in a circle, trying to figure out where she had vanished. In frustration, it lashed out at the scarecrow, tearing it to shreds and breaking the wooden pole.

The tip of Gwynevere's hat was swiped off and she swallowed a scream. This beast wasn't like the werewolves in Ashen. They were refined and sophisticated, capable of behaving just as they would every other day of the month during the full moon. Some of the more powerful ones could even change at will. Most importantly, they weren't hostile. This werewolf was vicious and raw, like a wild animal. The laws of Ashen were very strict about protecting their people from each other. Wherever this beast was from, it wasn't Ashen.

Gwynevere remained in shadow form until she was certain the werewolf had moved on. Once she felt safe, she readjusted her freshly lacerated hat and made her way toward the quiet little town. She needed to find the others, quickly.

"Mother," she whispered as she made her way through the cornfield. "If you can hear me—" her voice broke, "I can't do this alone." Her eyes filled with tears, she'd always had her parents to protect her, and guide her, and now.... She turned to the starry sky, "Father, are you guilty? You can't be. I beg and plead that you're not... please, give me a sign."

Gwynevere had just passed beneath a large knotted oak tree when she heard a squeak in the distance. Her heart leapt, and she dropped to her knees. "Samuel!" she cried out and scooped him up into her hands. "Always the best familiar," she said as she kissed his furry head. "You always seem to know how to find me."

The rat continued to squeak wildly. "Yes, I know! There was something really off about that guy," said Gwynevere referring to the werewolf. "Everyone is safe though, right?" Samuel squeaked and hopped out of her hands, hurrying toward the main part of town. "Oh, I see. Well, let's not keep them waiting."

Gwynevere followed the little rat familiar through the brush toward an old abandoned well, which sat behind the tumbled remnants of an old brick house. Miss Bigsby's shop stood just across the street. The werewolf's howl—carried by the wind—sent chills down Gwynevere's spine.

Samuel leapt atop the lip of the well and squeaked. Even though the top had been sealed closed by pieces of wood, she could still hear familiar voices. She cupped her hands around her mouth and called out. "Evelyn? Mr. Moody, are you down there?"

"That's her!" Evelyn cried out excitedly. "That's Gwynevere." She clutched Rufus to her chest and felt her father's hand on her shoulder. "Yes! Help us out." Her voice echoed up the dark well shaft.

Gwynevere breathed a sigh of relief. She ran her hand over the wood. "*Displacio*," she commanded. The old boards began to tremble and creak. Gwynevere took a step back as the wood exploded into shards. "Not quite what I expected," she muttered, brushing bits of wood from her clothing.

Evelyn took her father's hand and placed Rufus on her shoulder. "Father stand perfectly still."

"You're about to use your magic?" he asked, clearly nervous.

"Yes, Father," said Evelyn. "There's no need to be frightened. You can help me."

"How?" he whispered into the darkness.

"Just believe that you are weightless," she said softly. "Like a whisper."

"Weightless... got it," he nodded and closed his eyes.

The next thing he knew, he was slowly ascending up the well, pulled gently by his daughter's hand. They floated to the top of the well, settling down beside it.

Gwynevere hugged her sister, "That was brilliant." Samuel twitched his nose and squeaked in agreement.

"You got away from that dreadful creature unscathed?"

"Vampires are naturally adapted to outwit werewolves at every turn," stated Gwynevere proudly.

"I can scarcely believe such a horrific beast attacked us," said Thomas.

"We should get as far away from here as possible," Evelyn eyed her surroundings nervously.

"No," said Gwynevere. "If we do that, it will pick up our scent again and track us down. It's best if we stay local and lie low until morning. This breed of werewolf is not like the ones I know from home. When it is in its wolf form, it is much more feral."

Samuel stood on his hind legs and sniffed at a nearby house that connected to one of the buildings from the local market. Rufus sauntered over and meowed. "What is it, Samuel?"

"He's looking at Miss Bigsby's home," said Evelyn. "She is somewhat of a friend. We may be able to hide there. She sells a lot of food and spices that could mask our scent."

"Food and spices you say?" Gwynevere rubbed her chin. "Exactly what I need to make a potion. Though we are left without pixie dust…."

"I left the spell book back at the house," said Evelyn. "Maybe there's a chance—"

Eerie howls came from within the cornfield, moving closer. "He's coming!" whispered Mr. Moody, his eyes open wide with fear.

"This is no time to be neighborly," decided Gwynevere, "we must seek safety from your friend."

The group hurried to the back door of Miss Bigsby's home. Thomas followed, casting nervous glances over his shoulder. Evelyn cupped her hands around her mouth.

"Hello? Miss Bigsby?" she whispered as loudly as possible. "It's Evelyn Moody. We need your help."

Gwynevere rapped her knuckles on the door. To their surprise the door swung open with an agitated creak. The sisters stood in the doorway. Something seemed strangely wrong. Another howl filled the air, this time much closer. Thomas shoved the girls into the doorway, turned and locked the door. "We'll apologize for the intrusion when we find Miss Bigsby."

Rufus meowed in wholehearted agreement and began exploring the dark room.

Gwynevere sniffed the air. "The spices smell very strong in here. We may be safe unless the werewolf is willing to risk exposure to more people."

"You said yourself it acted more like an animal," whispered Thomas. "Leading me to assume it will not care."

Gwynevere sighed and shrugged. "We don't have any other choices at the moment."

"Hello? Miss Bigsby?" Evelyn called out. Only silence reached her ears, a sudden uneasiness washed over her. "Somebody find a light."

Gwynevere felt her hat brush against a hanging lamp, she reached up and steadied it to keep it from swaying back and forth. She whispered the word *luminous*—a small flame flickered to life within the glass globe of the lamp.

Their eyes widened as they realized why the smell was so strong. The room was in complete disarray. Ripped bags of spices were scattered about—their contents spread across the floor. Shattered pots lay beside an overturned table, a shelf hung precariously from the wall. Gwynevere gasped at the sight, noting a large slash mark on the wall by the door.

"Oh my God," Thomas whispered.

"Miss Bigsby?!" Evelyn cried out, fearing the worst. She eyed a set of stairs, concluding that they must lead to her bedroom. "Gwynevere—"

"I see them," she responded, hurrying toward the stairs. She turned to Mr. Moody. "Stay down here with Samuel and Rufus and keep an ear out."

"Don't linger too long," said Thomas. He shivered and looked around the destroyed living space. "My concerns are only growing by the minute."

Gwynevere nodded and crept up the stairs behind Evelyn. They reached the top and peered through the doorway into a bedroom that was even emptier than what Evelyn had known. A single bed had been dragged across the floor to the middle of the room. Shredded clothes were thrown about—drawers had been torn from an overturned wardrobe. Gwynevere peeked into the bathing room. The mirror was smashed, and the curtains were ripped to shreds.

"How well did you know Miss Bigsby?" asked Gwynevere, studying the room.

"Well enough," said Evelyn in a low voice. Her heart pounded as she searched the room for signs of a body. The claw marks on the wall did not bode well for Miss Bigsby. "She's very nice. She grows her own spices and... I had hoped that she and my father...."

"Did Thomas have feelings for her?" Gwynevere asked softly.

Evelyn nodded. "He's had his eye on her for some time, and I believe, she thought fondly of him as well. I had planned at one point to try and help things along a little," her cheeks blushed red. "You know, a little potion."

"She sounds lovely," Gwynevere smiled kindly. "I just hope—"

"I know," Evelyn replied, finishing her thought, "that somehow she survived."

"Why would the werewolf come after Miss Bigsby?"

Evelyn shook her head. "I have no idea. The only connection I see is that she was the one who told the town inspector that she sold me spices."

"The town inspector?" asked Gwynevere. "That boorish man that accosted you at your father's house?" Evelyn didn't answer, she didn't need too.

"Wait a second," Gwynevere clenched her fingers around Evelyn's arm.

Evelyn looked at her and yanked her arm back. "Hey careful," she grimaced, rubbing her arm. "You're really strong."

"What if the inspector knew I was here?" asked Gwynevere. "What if he could smell me from the first time I was there? If he smelt the magic I was using."

Evelyn looked at Gwynevere, her face filled with confusion. "But how would he be able to smell…," her eyes grew wide with realization. "Oh my God. The inspector of Yorkshire is a werewolf!"

Tap. Tap. Tap.

"It's Father!" He was tapping the ceiling beneath their feet. They hurried to the stairs, descending as quietly as possible.

"He's by the well," Thomas motioned frantically. "Follow me. I found the door to Miss Bigsby's cellar."

A shadow passed by the window. Without thought, Thomas and the girls dropped to the floor, crawling the rest of the way to the cellar door. Thomas reached up from his crouched position, found the handle and swung it open. Thankfully, it opened quietly without a squeaky rebuke from the old hinges. Heavy air—laden with the acrid smell of spices—assaulted his nostrils.

Thomas cast a wary eye at the window. "Hurry," he mouthed, waving the girls toward the stairs. Evelyn went first. She crept down the rickety stairs, grimacing as each step creaked and groaned under each footfall. Gwynevere followed close behind, her mind racing with options should the werewolf corner them in the cellar.

Thomas could hear the werewolf's agitated pacing outside the front door. It's raspy breathing and whines sent chills down his spine. He shooed Rufus and Samuel into the cellar, and then followed behind them. No sooner had he turned to slide the lock into place, the werewolf attacked the house with such ferocity that the whole house shook.

Rufus leapt from the cellar floor to Evelyn's shoulder. Samuel raced up Gwynevere's legs and torso, not slowing until he burrowed himself in her hair, beneath her torn hat. Streams of light bled through the cracks in the flooring above. Clouds of dust shimmered and sparkled gold in the glowing beams. Thomas held a finger to his lips, his eyes wide with fear.

Gwynevere prayed that the smell of spices would be enough to hide their scents. Her eyes roamed across the room, searching for anything that could be used as a weapon, but all she could see were rows of glass jars and various sacks, stacked against the walls. Evelyn pressed her shoulder against her, trembling.

For a moment, everything was still. Had the creature given up? Samuel poked his head out from beneath Gwynevere's hat and twitched his nose. Evelyn closed her eyes, listening intently. It was at the exact moment when hope began to fill her heart when the werewolf burst into the house, the door toppling to the floor like a felled tree. Enraged, the beast tromped around the room, snorting and sniffing, slashing at curtains and pictures. It snorted loudly, its whimpering becoming shriller by the second.

Thomas wrapped his arms around his daughter, silently praying for their safety. Like a magnet drawn to steel, his eyes were riveted to the cellar door. Evelyn reached out for Gwynevere's hand. There was no way they would survive an attack against a feral werewolf.

The beast scurried up the stairs to Miss Bigsby's bedroom, its claws making scraping, scratching noises as it climbed. The werewolf pawed at its snout and whimpered with frustration. It clambered down the stairs back into the main room. Dust fell between the boards onto the girls and Thomas, directly below where the werewolf stood. The beast lowered its nose to the floorboards and sniffed.

Gwynevere balled her hands into fists and clenched her jaws. She wasn't going down without a fight.

Evelyn buried her head in her father's chest. Why was fate so cruel? She'd just learned of her sister, and now....

The werewolf was moving again. Its shadow passed in front of the cellar door and stopped. Thomas held his breath, his hand threaded through Evelyn's hair, pulling her tight against his chest. He knew that he would fight to the death to protect her. The beast released a hellish snarl, then turned, and raced out into the night.

The trio remained motionless and silent for another moment and then turned to face each other. "Is he gone?" whispered Evelyn.

"I think so," said Gwynevere softly. "It was as if something scared it away."

"Or, the smell of the spice worked," said Evelyn in an excited whisper.

Thomas moved away from the girls and slumped down against a sack of pepper. After a moment, he let out a heavy sigh. "Well, this couldn't have possibly gone worse."

"Couldn't have gone worse? Have you heard of death? I think that would have been worse," Gwynevere stated. "A feral werewolf wouldn't take us to prison."

Thomas studied Gwynevere's ruby-red vampire eyes that gave a faint red glow in the darkness. "I suppose you're proof of the difference between legend and fact," he said.

"What do you mean?" asked Gwynevere.

"A vampire that isn't a bloodsucker."

Gwynevere felt a flash of anger. "Bloodsucker is a derogatory term and I'd appreciate you not using it."

"I see, I apologize," he shifted uncomfortably. "I didn't know."

"Fair enough," Gwynevere's voice softened. "You're correct, vampires drink blood. My father needed blood to survive. However, he never turned on anyone and sucked their blood. He bought it and kept it from coagulating until he needed it. Because I am half-witch, I do not require blood as subsistence."

"Thank you for explaining," he smiled, then turned to his daughter, "And now, I guess there's quite a bit of explaining that I owe you." Evelyn looked at her father curiously. "I don't want you to think it was because I *wanted* to lie to you. I simply—"

"Wanted to protect me," Evelyn sighed. "I know, Father," she stood and wrapped her arms around him. "I understand why you did what you did, and believe me, I'm just as terrified about what happened to Miss

Bigsby. What happened to my mom… what might happen to my sister…."

"Hey, nothing is going to get me without a fight," said Gwynevere. "Right, Samuel?"

Right, he squeaked with affirmation.

9 - Memories

Evelyn laid her head back. The stone wall felt good on the back of her head and neck. The events of the evening had sapped her of all of her energy. She watched her father, who was staring at his feet, caught up within his own thoughts.

"Dad, did you love my mom?"

"What? Yes," he answered emphatically, "very much so."

"Oh," Gwynevere cooed excitedly, "I want to know all about this." She wrapped Samuel up in her arms and squeezed him tight, much to his dismay.

"Alright," sighed Thomas, "but where to start?"

"That's easy, start with how you two met," Evelyn suggested.

"Oh, oh, *and* fall in love," giggled Gwynevere.

Thomas laughed and held up his calloused hands, "Okay, give me a moment to gather my thoughts." He closed his eyes as a flood of memories filled his head. "My father died when I was a young man. He ran a store selling textiles and other goods. It never did well. My father wasn't much of a salesman, and when he passed, I inherited a shop that was heavy in debt."

"What about your mother?" asked Gwynevere.

"She left when I was seven. She wasn't cut out for the living meal-by-meal lifestyle."

"Oh, I'm sorry for asking."

Thomas waved her comment away. "I was so angry at my mother for leaving and not taking me with her, and my father for dying and leaving me in debt. I took the little bit of money that I had and drank myself into a stupor each night, and that's how I met Adelaide."

"You met her at a bar, Father?!" Evelyn cried aghast at the thought. Rufus made a sound deep in his throat, obviously offended as well.

"No. No." Thomas shook his head. "I was walking back to my shop. It was *freezing* outside—"

"And you fell in a lake and using her magical powers, she saved you from drowning?" Gwynevere asked excitedly, sliding closer.

"Where do you get this imagination? None of that happened." His cheeks flushed red. "Do you want me to tell the story or not?"

"Yes," Gwynevere nodded, "I'm sorry for interrupting."

"Where was I?"

"Freezing, Father," Evelyn helped him along.

"Oh, yes. I made it to the doorstep and passed out. Had Adelaide not found me, I would have frozen to death."

"And she fell in love with you and had a child? I always thought my mother had higher expectations, no offense Evelyn."

"None taken," she laughed, rubbing her fingers around Rufus's ears.

"Your mother was the one who turned my life around. She told me in no uncertain terms how foolish I was being and that's when we made a pact."

"A pact?" Evelyn looked at her father quizzically.

"Your mother," he shook his head, "not only was she beautiful, but she had a heart of gold. She promised that if I turned my life around, that she would *have* to come see me more often. I still remember that mischievous glint in those dazzling blue eyes."

Gwynevere was pretty sure that Rufus looked up from Evelyn's lap and rolled his eyes.

"Father," Evelyn cried, her cheeks turning bright red. "Did you do what she asked?"

"Like a hopeless fool in love," Thomas laughed unabashedly.

Warmth coursed through Evelyn's veins, it had been years since she'd seen her father laugh. Rufus purred and buried his head in her lap.

"I put everything I had into my shop until I was making a steady profit. The name Moody became well-known all through Yorkshire." His eyes visited a place far away. His chest rose and fell with the memories. "Did you know that I was given a special award from the Mayor?"

"No, Father," Evelyn smiled, "I'm so proud of you."

"Yes," he said. "I was single-handedly responsible for bringing more traffic to the small town."

"I wish I could have seen that," she rubbed her father's arm, wishing he could be that man again.

"I can remember so vividly when I saw your mother again. I'd just placed the broom in the corner, and was about to lock the door when she appeared. I thanked her for everything she'd done for me. She placed her hand on my heart and told me, 'A life worth living, is a life worth saving.'"

Thomas looked at Gwynevere and smiled. "The moment I saw you, deep inside I knew who you were. The hat that you're wearing. I made it for your mother."

"Really...?" said Gwynevere. She touched the brim of her hat. "I always thought it was just a hat."

Thomas laughed, "That hat is actually number thirty-seven. It took me that many times to get it right."

"So," Evelyn knotted her fingers together, she knew she had come to the point of the story where all of their lives had changed. "I guess you and Mom fell in love, and then I was born?"

Thomas let out a heavy sigh. "One night, your mother told me where she really came from. A place called Ashen. It was law that we never coexist or interact. Our worlds were supposedly sealed off from one another. That is until Adelaide discovered a way in."

Thomas was quiet for a long time. He stared at his hands, rubbing his thumb over his fingers in nervous circles. Evelyn took her father's rough hands in hers, "It's okay, Father. I understand."

"No, Evelyn, it's only fair that you should know the truth. You've waited long enough. When your mother told me she was pregnant, I was over the moon. I told your mother it had been my dream to have a family. The next morning, when I awoke, she was gone."

"She left you?" whispered Evelyn. She couldn't believe how much pain her father had suffered.

"Six months later, there was a knock at my door. Imagine my surprise," Thomas's voice broke, "when I found a baby girl on my doorstep." Tears welled in his eyes, spilling down his cheeks. "A note pinned to your blanket said: Take care of her."

"And you did," Evelyn declared in earnest, "Very well in fact."

"I did my best," he smiled. "You're so much like your mother, it's uncanny. You are the greatest gift that anyone has ever given me."

"Now I understand why Mother never seemed as happy as I knew she wanted to be," said Gwynevere. "Her and Father were always fighting—only kind to each other when I was around."

"You were probably the only one that brought Mom true happiness," said Evelyn kindly.

"Please don't misunderstand me," Gwynevere insisted. "They both treated me well, but they were happiest when they were apart from one another."

"I hate to even ask this," said Evelyn tentatively, "but do you think that was enough motive for, uhm… well…."

"No, I mean, I don't know. My father never raised a hand to Mother. They may have argued, but I never saw even a hint of violence."

"So, now what do we do? If Father and I stay here in Yorkshire…."

"Don't worry, I have a plan." Rufus looked up from Evelyn's lap and meowed as if to say, *You do?* Samuel crawled down to Gwynevere's shoulder and squeaked. "Tonight we'll have to stay here. Once morning comes, we'll be protected from any feral werewolves. Then we'll figure a way back to Ashen."

"Ashen?" Thomas and Evelyn chorused.

"Yes. At this point there is only one powerful witch that can help us."

"And who might that be?" asked Evelyn.

"Mama Maggie, our grandmother."

10 - Bones

The morning sun shimmered around the edges of the cellar door. A songbird tweeted its morning lullaby from a nearby tree. Gwynevere stretched out over sacks of flour and wheat, turned away from the sunlight and faced the stone wall, drooling from her mouth as she snored.

Thomas stirred awake as Rufus gently nuzzled his stubbly cheek, purring loudly. He stretched and stood up slowly. "Okay, okay, Rufus," he muttered. "I'm up." Rufus turned to the others and meowed loudly. "I assume you're telling me to wake them up as well."

Thomas clomped up the stairs, slid the lock, and pushed the cellar door open. Golden sunlight spilled into the room. Evelyn groaned and shifted in her spot. "Why?" she moaned covering her face with her hand. *What am I laying on?* She rubbed her eyes and twisted her body, coming face to face with a human skull. "AHHH!" she screamed, flinging herself onto the ground and rolling away.

Rufus dashed across the room and leapt on top of Evelyn. Gwynevere sprung off the sacks of flour, landing in a low crouch, ready to do battle. "Why is everyone…? Ahh!" Gwynevere yelled, lifted Evelyn off the floor and threw her to her father. Thomas managed to throw up his arms just as the two collided with a thud against the cellar stairs.

"Don't tell me I just spent the night with that thing!" Evelyn cried out as she untangled herself from her father. "And Gwynevere, stop grabbing me and stop throwing me! You're really strong! *Think* before you *do*!"

"Sorry," said Gwynevere panting, "I was trying to protect you."

"By hurling me across the room like a bale of hay? Less protecting, okay? I'd like to at least make it to thirty."

"Okay, okay. I'm sorry. A simple thank you would have sufficed."

Evelyn dusted her dress off and slowly approached the skeleton. Samuel parted Gwynevere's hair like a curtain and peeked out. *Squeak, squeak.*

"No," said Gwynevere, "I don't think that's Miss Bigsby." The bones were mostly intact, wrapped in a dirtied, burnt garment.

"Gwynevere's right," nodded Thomas. "That corpse is nothing but bone. How long must one be kept in a cellar to decay into such a state?"

Evelyn shuttered. "Clearly the werewolf—"

"Werewolves do not do this," said Gwynevere. "I've known plenty of werewolves my whole life. Not even a feral wolf would do this. This is…," she breathed out slowly. "This is why my father could never go out in the sun."

"What do you mean?!" exclaimed Evelyn.

"Look," said Gwynevere. She pointed to the two very prominent fangs in the mouth of the skeleton. "This vampire," she rubbed a remnant of the singed clothing between her fingers, "was burnt alive under the sun."

"I thought vampires burning up in the sun was a myth," gasped Evelyn. "Like Lord Ruthven. You know, from Polidori's novel. Or you, you don't burn."

"I'm a half-vampire, I'm immune," explained Gwynevere. "And Lord Ruthven is a character from a novel. A full-blooded vampire will die if they are exposed to the sun for long periods of time."

"And that's what you think happened to this poor woman," Evelyn asked, horrified by the idea.

"Yes," said Gwynevere somberly.

"That's… horrible," said Thomas.

"Yes… but why is her body here?" asked Gwynevere.

"Was Miss Bigsby a vampire?" asked Evelyn. "Seems like a peculiar thing to keep in your cellar."

"If she was, you would have known," said Gwynevere. "We can't hide our appearances the same way werewolves can. They look like ordinary townsfolk in their human form. Maybe just a little hairier."

"Tell me, are werewolves dangerous in their human forms?" asked Thomas.

"No, their abilities are greatly diminished when they're transformed. A word of caution though, there are those that are so powerful, they can turn into their human form at will."

"We need to confront Inspector Morgan in the safety of daylight and find out *why* he tried to kill us." Thomas crossed his arms confidently.

Evelyn stared at her father. He seemed renewed, invigorated. This was a side of her father she'd rarely seen. "I'm proud of you, Father."

Thomas pulled Evelyn into his arms. He looked at Gwynevere and smiled. "I want you to know that no matter what happens, I consider you family."

"Thank you. That means a lot, Mr. Moody," she flicked her fangs out of habit and smiled. "It seems that we are surrounded by mystery. Who killed Mother? What happened to my father and why is the inspector trying to kill us?"

"Don't forget this poor being." Evelyn nodded toward the skeleton. "It seems that werewolves and vampires are crossing over from Ashen, and we have no idea how, how many, and for how long."

Gwynevere looked back at the skeleton. The familiars were busily sniffing about. Rufus turned his gaze to the young witch and let out a long meow. "Yeah, yeah, no one is blaming you. No one could smell it with all the spices down here." Samuel squeaked in agreement.

"We've much to do," said Evelyn. "One of us should go back and get Mother's book."

"I'll do that," offered Gwynevere. "If there are people there, I can slip it out unnoticed. I'll need it to help me get back to Ashen so I can speak with Mama Maggie."

"Wait," Evelyn cried, "you're not going back permanently, are you?"

"Permanently?" Gwynevere reached out and took her sister's hand. "I wouldn't dream of it."

Evelyn embraced her and then held her by the shoulders. "You better be careful." She arched an eyebrow and then hugged Gwynevere again.

"Now where's the fun in that?" Gwynevere smiled mischievously.

"Come on, Rufus," Evelyn called out. "It's time to go."

The stairs creaked and groaned under Thomas's feet. Rufus bolted across the floor and padded up the stairs at Evelyn's heels. She turned and smiled at Gwynevere, then followed her father out the door.

An unusual sensation warmed Gwynevere's heart. Finding acceptance from a man like Mr. Moody meant more to her than she thought it would. It was strange seeing a man that cared so much for her mother and equally so for his daughter. It was an emotional connection she'd never shared with her father. Samuel squeaked at her. She reached down and scratched behind his ears.

Gwynevere's eyes moved from Samuel to the skeletal remains. "Who are you?" She inspected the clothing as Samuel moved up and down the skeleton sniffing about. She looked at her familiar expectantly. "Anything?"

Samuel scrunched his face and wriggled his nose. *Squeak, squeak.* "You smell hyacinth?" Gwynevere whispered. "That's odd." She rubbed her chin and flicked her fangs. The scent seemed so familiar. There was something lumpy beneath the black fabric that had melted like glue over the bones of the fingers. Gwynevere scraped at the molten material with her thumbnail, revealing a sliver of gold. "A ring," the young witch whispered.

Samuel leapt from the canvas bag onto her waist and scurried up her body to her shoulder. *Squeak, squeak.* "You're right," said Gwynevere, dropping the skeletal hand. "We've got to get that spell book from Mr. Moody's before anyone else finds it." Samuel squeaked in agreement. "Hopefully, Mother gave some clues as to how to return home in that book...."

"Where is everyone?" asked Thomas, not expecting an answer. He raised his hand, shading his eyes from the bright morning sunlight and scouted the town. By this time of the day, the streets of Yorkshire would be bustling, but there wasn't a soul anywhere to be seen.

"Father, the streetlights are still burning." Rufus's ears were pinned to his head, and his tail twitched nervously. "I'm starting to feel uneasy here."

"Maybe the town hall enforced a lockdown because of the werewolf. Keep a keen eye out for Inspector Morgan," warned Thomas.

Evelyn didn't need to be told. Her eyes flicked left and right inspecting every shadow. Rufus meowed and dipped his head. "He said the beast went this way."

"I'm not sure anyone is here. The windows are boarded up and barred...."

"Maybe Inspector Morgan had everyone evacuate, especially if he knew he wasn't able to control himself," Evelyn suggested.

Rufus came to a stop in front of the town hall building and gave a single low meow. Evelyn eyed the slender red brick building warily. "Rufus said he's inside," whispered Evelyn.

Thomas simply nodded and headed for the door. Rufus matched his stride step for step. He paused on the stoop and turned to Evelyn. "Stay behind me. If anything happens, run." He placed a hand on her shoulder. "Promise me," he demanded.

"I promise," she lied, knowing that she could never leave her father behind.

On trembling legs, Thomas climbed the steps to the town hall building. His fingers circled the brass door handle, warmed by the sun. He pushed, and the door swung open easily. Rufus brushed past his legs and meowed for them to follow. Just as Evelyn stepped inside, Rufus arched his back and growled angrily.

"I wouldn't do that if I were you," spoke a familiar voice from the darkness.

Evelyn gasped as Inspector Morgan stepped out of the shadows. He looked at Evelyn and her father with disdain.

"You! You tried to kill us last night!" she pointed an accusatory finger at the man, barely able to contain the rage consuming her.

"Easy, dear," said Thomas. "Please, let me handle this."

"Having trouble keeping that *leash* on your child, Thomas Moody?" scoffed Inspector Morgan.

"Do not disrespect my daughter," Thomas hissed as he slowly approached the inspector. The inspector cocked his head to the side, a smug look on his face. He was apparently amused that a mere mortal dared to challenge him. Rufus arched his back and snarled angrily.

"No, Rufus," scolded Evelyn. She scooped him up and cradled him in her arms. "Instead of being a smarmy toad, why don't you tell us what's going on here."

"All in due time." The inspector took a step toward Evelyn, and Thomas stepped between them, who crossed his arms and set his jaw. "Mr. Moody, if you would please step aside. I need to take your daughter in for questioning."

"I'm not going anywhere with you!" Evelyn cried out. "You tried to kill us!"

"I did no such thing. I do assure you however, if I wanted to kill you…," he stared at Evelyn, allowing her to fill in the blanks. "You must come with me now before I lose my patience. I've been yearning to leave this godforsaken countryside for good, and today is that day. Now!"

Evelyn stared him down. "I'm not going anywhere with you," she hissed. The stone floor rumbled beneath their feet, cracks zigzagged like lightning, threatening to topple the building. Her eyes began to glow like magnificent orbs of white light. Massive chunks of stone rose from the floor and swirled around her. Thomas and the inspector both watched in awe.

"Evelyn!" her father cried out. "Evelyn, what are you doing?!"

A whisper of ancient tongue escaped Evelyn's lips. She motioned toward the inspector, and the stones rocketed through the air at him.

Inspector Morgan thrust his hands forward—the stones hung in the air, then dropped to the ground at his feet. "Enough!" he cried. He sliced his arm through the air as if holding an invisible sword, Evelyn and her father were swept off their feet and slammed into the back wall.

"Dad," Evelyn moaned, climbing to her hands and knees, "Are you okay?"

"Yes, I'm fine. Get out of here. You promised me," his voice broke as he struggled to his feet.

Rufus hissed at the inspector, baring his fangs.

"Tsk. Tsk. Rufus. You've done well. I promised I wouldn't harm them, and aside from a few scrapes and bruises, I have kept my word."

"Rufus! What is he talking about? What promise?" Evelyn couldn't understand what was happening. "What is going on?!" she demanded.

Rufus gazed sadly into Evelyn's eyes—eyes filled with hurt, confusion, betrayal. Her familiar meowed softly.

"What did he say?" asked Thomas.

"Inspector Morgan is not the werewolf." Evelyn's voice was barely above a whisper. "He's a powerful warlock... and he's been spying on me for all this time."

"Listen, child, there is a lot going on that you don't understand. The werewolf wasn't sent here for you. He was sent to return your mysterious friend to Ashen. I evacuated everyone from the town to make sure they were safe, and the apprehension went uninterrupted."

"That mysterious friend is my sister!" shouted Evelyn. "And if you lay a single finger on her I'll—"

Morgan sighed and shook his head, cutting her off. "I do not have time for this." He turned his attention to Rufus. The cat nodded and meowed solemnly. "Perhaps you're right."

Evelyn began crying. She clutched her father's arm and pulled him against her. "Rufus, why would you betray us?" she wailed. "Rufus?!"

Morgan's eyes began to glow. He raised his right hand toward the sky and cried, "Exveilitoramas!"

There was a blinding flash of light that consumed the entire village block. The light vanished as quickly as it came, along with the Moody family, the false inspector, leaving not a trace of anyone within the old ghost town of Yorkshire.

11 - Family

Yep, thought Gwynevere, *Mr. Moody's shop had definitely been attacked by a werewolf.* She felt a twang of guilt. "You know, Samuel, none of this would have happened if I hadn't come here." Samuel twitched his whiskers and nodded in agreement.

The front door barely clung to the doorframe, secured by a single hinge, like fingers hanging to the edge of a cliff. *Squeak, squeak.* "That's right," nodded Gwynevere, "thank you." Samuel reminded her that Evelyn had blocked the front entrance.

Gwynevere hopped off the front stoop and walked around the shop to the shattered second-story window. She levitated, rotated in the air, then floated into the room. It was a disaster. Evelyn's bed was shredded. Broken boxes were scattered across the room, their contents smashed. It looked as if a twister had touched down in the middle of the room. Glass crunched beneath her shoes. "Please, please be here." She leapt over the shredded mattress and whispered a sigh of relief. Her mother's book lay on the floor unscathed, behind the bed.

Gwynevere carefully brushed off the cover. A feeling of calmness swept over her as she held something so dear to her mother and sister. She opened the book and ran her fingers over the rough parchment and handwritten etchings. It was almost exactly like the book she had back at home. She wished that Evelyn had been able to know her mother—she was remarkable. Samuel gently squeaked. "You're right my friend. I need to find the conflux potions."

She flipped through the pages until she came to a section filled with notes in her mother's handwriting. "Here it is, Samuel! I found it." Samuel opened his mouth as if to say, *Oh!* "Alright, think of the place you wish to be, and say *exveilitoramas.*"

Gwynevere found herself standing in her bedroom. All she could recall was a flash of light, and then she was here.

Samuel squeaked excitedly, leapt from her shoulder and nestled himself into an open drawer next to Gwynevere's bed. She looked around her gothic-inspired bedroom, and then thought of her sister's room, bare and sparse. She hung her head feeling like a spoiled rich girl.

"Come on, Samuel. It's been a long time since we practiced our broom skills. We've got to get to Mama Maggie's house, she'll know what to do." Samuel looked at her wide-eyed, gave a nervous squeak, and then wriggled out of sight, burying himself between the folds of a blanket. "What are you afraid of silly rat?" *Squeak, squeak,* replied Samuel, his explanation muffled by the blanket. "Of course I can fly, I'm just a little out of practice."

Gwynevere hurried down the hall to where her mother kept her brooms. There were fast-flying brooms, long-distance brooms and even tandem brooms made for two people. She decided on a black-handled broom with bristles shaped like a fuselage of a rocket. Gwynevere had yet to be properly trained in the art of flight but she shrugged to Samuel, how difficult could it be? If rickety old witches could zip around the sky on them, so could she.

Gwynevere straddled the broom, leaned forward and kicked off with her feet. She was hurled backward as the broom rocketed skyward. Samuel clung to her dress—his whiskers flattened against his face. She fought to get the unruly besom under control. She leaned downward on the tip and sent them plummeting. Samuel squeaked loudly in her ear. "Don't you think I know that?!" she shouted angrily.

Gwynevere managed to right the broom, after succeeding in only breaking a few tree limbs from the sacred oak outside the council hall. If her arrival to Ashen had been a secret, it certainly wasn't anymore. Unfortunately, Dolly was outside watering the hyacinths at the government building when Gwynevere rocketed overhead. Several of the Mayor's personally appointed police officers raced outside the council hall to investigate. Dolly stepped aside as one of the men began barking orders. These were no ordinary police officers—they were scouts and trackers. She knew it was only a matter of time before Gwynevere would be captured. Dolly dropped her water pail with a clang and hurried back inside.

"Slow down! Slow down!" Gwynevere cried as she tore through a flock of birds nearly impaling one with the handle of her broom. She slowed and gained control, her feet dangling nearly seventy-five feet off the ground. Samuel climbed onto her shoulder and bit her ear. "Ouch!" Gwynevere yelled. Samuel squeaked loudly, raising his tiny paw in a fist. "Yeah, yeah, I know," she grumbled, "so much for low profile."

It had been a long time since she had been to Mama Maggie's house. She hoped she remembered how to get there. She closed her eyes, envisioning the blue-gold, glowing mushrooms that led up the walkway to her home.

The broom began moving on its own, sweeping and swooshing along the currents of the wind. Gwynevere smiled, feeling the connection with the broom—the energy ran through her body. Suddenly, the handle tilted downward, and they began descending rapidly. Gwynevere leaned backward on the broom laughing, her silvery white hair danced in the wind.

Just as she was about to touch down, Samuel squeaked loudly and launched himself from her shoulder into a thatch of clover. He landed with a thud, rolled head over tail and leapt to his feet unleashing a tirade of squeaks that no respectable woman would ever repeat. Gwynevere hopped from the broom, and shook her head at Samuel, "Don't be so dramatic!"

Gwynevere looked around. She had landed in a small clearing in the enchanted forest. Samuel stood on his hind feet, his whiskers twitching. He took two giant sniffs. *This way*, he squeaked. He scurried ahead, following his nose.

"Wait up! You crazy rat!" Gwynevere gave chase, scrambling through the leaf-covered forest, clawing through spiderwebs and underbrush. Samuel popped up through a fern and began squeaking excitedly. *Mushrooms! Mushrooms!*

"I see them!" A glowing path of mushrooms sprouted from a steep descent leading to a massive open grove where a squat cottage sat like a pumpkin. "Grandma's home," whispered Gwynevere excitedly.

She ran down the hill, clutching her broom tightly. Samuel scampered ahead of her, darting along to and fro. With one mighty leap, he landed on the porch and waited for Gwynevere to arrive. Seconds later, she too hopped onto the rickety landing, and then— wasting no time—she rapped her knuckles on the wooden door. Samuel, clambered onto her foot, ran up her legs and torso and hid beneath the rim of her hat.

"Who goes there?!" The angry voice was old and brittle. "Go away! I want nothing to do with you!"

Gwynevere paused, *Maybe this isn't a good idea. No, this has to be done.* She knocked again. "Mama Maggie?! It's Gwynevere!" she shouted.

"Gwynevere?! What are you doing out here in my woods?!" she could hear the old woman tromping about inside her house.

"It's a very long story! May I come in?!"

After a long silence, the door slowly creaked open on its own. Gwynevere fought to control her nerves. The truth was, she hardly knew anything about her grandmother. Not her doing, but her mother's. Adelaide and Mama Maggie never got along. Gwynevere had no idea why. But none of that was important right now. She needed answers. Petty family arguments would have to be cast aside. Right now, she needed an ally—someone to help protect her from the Mayor and his werewolf police, who at this moment were most likely searching for her. She also had her sister and Mr. Moody to worry about. Time was of the essence.

"Well? Come on in, girl. Don't just stand there collecting cobwebs."

Gwynevere knew her grandmother wasn't one for pleasantries. Her words were sharp, like the cracking of a dry stick. A shiver ran down her spine as she stepped through the doorway.

"Step in further, child. Your dear Mama Maggie can barely walk as it is."

Gwynevere took another step into the cottage—a pungent aroma filled her lungs. *I hope that's not dinner.* She jumped as the door shut and locked behind her. She pattered through the house, following her nose. Her grandmother was dressed in classical witch attire, a long black robe, a droopy black hat and shaggy hair that nearly covered the entirety of her face. As to be expected, Mama Maggie was busily stirring a bubbling vomitous green brew.

"Well, come closer, dear. Let me get a look at you," she motioned Gwynevere over with long, slender fingers. The candles in the room brightened. Mama Maggie grasped her granddaughter's hand. A crystal blue eye and crooked smile peeked out from behind her matted hair.

"Grandmother, there's a lot I need to tell you." Gwynevere paused, feeling the heaviness of loss in her heart again.

Mama Maggie turned her full attention to Gwynevere. "Please, take a seat," she said softly, gesturing to an old wooden table, accompanied by two chairs. "Does your mother know you're here?"

Such a simple question, thought Gwynevere as she fought back the tears. *I wish she did, that would mean she was still... alive.* "Mama Maggie," her voice caught in her throat, "she's dead." The word *dead* felt like a crushing blow, like a hammer striking a nail, driving it deep into a piece of wood.

Mama Maggie gasped and clutched the edge of her brewing table. "I... see...," she said in a heavy whisper. "Tell me child... what happened to my dear Adelaide?"

"I'm not sure," the sight of her mother's lifeless face filled her eyes. "She was murdered," Gwynevere whispered. "The Mayor thinks my father and I had something to do with it."

"Mayor Wimbly? Utter foolishness," the old witch scoffed. "I never once voted for that tired old dog."

Gwynevere fiddled with her fingers nervously. She could feel the power emanating from the old witch. Samuel remained hidden beneath her hair, listening curiously. "Well, continue child," Mama Maggie prompted, "tell me everything, every detail."

"Yes, Grandma," she smiled faintly. She felt a sense of relief overtake her, she'd made the right decision to come here. "Two days ago, Samuel and I were working on a potion for my mother. As usual, my mother was being secretive as to the purpose of the potion—which of course added to the excitement."

"Oh. And what *exactly* were you brewing?" Mama Maggie leaned in. Her eyes danced with curiosity.

"A complex mixture," said Gwynevere. "It required a drop of my blood, pure blood," she clarified.

"I see," said Mama Maggie quietly. "That means that the potion was meant specifically for you. Only you."

"Because of my blood?"

"Oh child," Mama Maggie tsked. "What did Adelaide teach you? How could you ever attend Ashen Academy if you don't even know the basics," she scoffed.

Gwynevere blinked back a surge of anger, how dare she speak of her mother this way.

"Blood is very sacred," continued Mama Maggie, "it's a very old ingredient from an even older form of magic called blood magic. Which, by the way, is illegal in Ashen, unless a very strict series of rules and regulations are followed."

"Illegal?" Gwynevere had a difficult time imagining her mother doing anything illegal. "You said there were rules and regulations, I'm quite sure Mother would have followed all of those."

"I would hope so. It's a powerful concoction," Mama Maggie arched her eyebrow. "The Ashen council banned the use of blood magic over half a millennia ago—too powerful for any common witch citizen to wield. The magic was, believe it or not, of vampiric origin."

"Woah," Gwynevere gasped in awe. "Do you think that because I'm a half-blood—"

"The potion would be much more potent. More so than Adelaide could have imagined. That woman," Mama Maggie clucked in disapproval, "always set her ambitions far above her skill level. And to use her *daughter's* blood in a magical brew…," she shook her head. "I can only imagine her intentions."

Gwynevere was confused. Her mother had been killed, and her grandmother seemed more interested in the conflux potion than her own daughter. "What do you mean by her intentions?"

"Depends." She let the word hang uncomfortably in the air. "Why don't you tell me what else was in that brew of yours," Mama Maggie smiled oddly.

"Nothing out of the ordinary, I assure you. Tail of a purple newt, a dash of rat whiskers, pixie dust as per the usual base. A few hours to boil and stir."

"Oh really?" Her grandmother made no attempt to hide her disbelief. "I find it hard to imagine that your little friend would be okay with the use of whiskers taken from his kin to fuel what sounds like a base mixture to some kind of consumable."

Samuel danced about Gwynevere's shoulder squeaking. "Yes, yes, I'll tell her," she assured the agitated familiar. "We don't use *actual* rat whiskers. There are far more humane alternatives."

"Alternatives," Mama Maggie scoffed. "I'm just fuming, knowing what Adelaide put you through without you even knowing. Continue with your story. I won't interrupt anymore if I can help it."

Gwynevere felt like she'd taken a punch to the gut. Until now, she hadn't realized the depth of the animosity between her mother and grandmother. The words stung. How could Mama Maggie speak so bitterly of her own daughter? "I'm not sure what to say…," she stared into the eyes of the old woman.

"I see," said Mama Maggie softly, "I've hurt your feelings. Pay no attention to the terse words of an old woman. Sometimes I let my tongue venture off on its own. We're family my little droplet of blood… you can tell me anything."

"It's okay… so, I took the potion to the house, but Mother and Father were fighting. They fought a lot," Gwynevere explained. "Anyways, Father asked me to deliver a letter to Mayor Wimbly."

"I thought your father hated the Mayor." Mama Maggie cocked an eyebrow as if to say, *Am I wrong?*

"I don't think my father ever hated anyone," Gwynevere disappeared into her thoughts for a moment. "My dad was… unusual to say the least, but he was never cruel. He simply had a unique way of expressing himself. But he did care for me, my mother and for others."

"Hah," snorted the old witch. "Mayor Wimbly did everything within his power to unseat your father from his position on the council. I can assure you that your father felt nothing but malice toward the Mayor."

"Unseat? Are you sure?" questioned Gwynevere. "Father said the feud stemmed from old vampire and werewolf rivalries, nothing more. I believe my father and Judge Aiden were the only two vampires on the council, and she is highly respected. And she's an emissary for the Academy."

"Judge Aiden was a nuisance to the Academy during the time I ran as the head chairman," Mama Maggie scowled. "She wanted to push you along like a toddler behind the scenes for the sake of your father, at the cost of my integrity. I couldn't allow that."

"She did?" Gwynevere was shocked by the revelation. "Wait, you were the head chairman at the Ashen Academy?"

"Of course," Mama Maggie said indignantly. "What did Adelaide teach you? You don't rise to my level by memorizing basic spells and potion puffery," she sniffed. "There are but a handful of great witches and warlocks that have achieved my skill level." She readjusted her hat and brushed her scraggly hair from her face. "Age," she frowned. "Age caused me to retire, and for that, I will forever be bitter at Father Time for not granting me another century of youth."

Gwynevere shifted in her seat and smiled. "Well, I think you look great." Samuel squeaked in agreement. "I'm sorry, I never knew that much about you—"

"Yes," Mama Maggie spat out the word. "Adelaide never wanted you to know anything about me. She believed I would be a negative influence on you. *Imagine*," she screeched. "She shut me out, cast me aside from my own family, my own granddaughter. But the past is in the past, and I have rambled on—tell me, what did you do when you came home and found your mother?"

Gwynevere hesitated, "Found my mother? Who said I found my mother when I returned?" She shifted in her seat nervously.

"Oh," Mama Maggie shrugged, "I just assumed. You run off to take the letter to the Mayor, you return, and Adelaide is…," she looked down her nose at Gwynevere, "dead."

"Actually, it was later that night. I had just fallen asleep when I heard a series of loud…," Gwynevere tilted her head to the side trying to figure out the right word, "…bumps. There was a series of bumps, and then it was quiet. I tiptoed down the hall and found my mother… lying dead in her room."

Gwynevere shuddered—there was something unsettling about her grandmother's behavior. She worked her tongue around in her mouth, it felt so dry. "I called the police, but the strange thing is, when they arrived, the Mayor and his assistant came too. He sent me back to my room and placed a guard at my door. I thought he was trying to protect me, but then he told me that he thought my father and I had conspired to kill her." Gwynevere's heart pounded—would Mama Maggie know she'd twisted the truth?

The old witch stared at Gwynevere, an odd look in her eyes. She leaned forward resting her hands on the brewing table. "He thought you killed your mother?"

"Yes. He wanted to take me in for questioning. But something didn't feel right. I used my shadow magic, slipped out my bedroom window and hid behind the brewing house." Gwynevere swallowed hard seeing the questioning look in Mama Maggie's eyes. She hoped that twisting lies with the truth would satiate her grandmother's suspicions. "Mother kept the shack away from the house because of the smell," Gwynevere explained. "It threw off the Mayor's werewolves, and I hid there until I thought it was safe to escape and find you."

"And that was it?" she asked curiously. "You just... hid... until you came here?"

"Yes," Gwynevere lied. Her fingers fidgeted at the top of her dress, pulling it away from her neck. She glanced away, afraid her grandmother would see the deceit in her eyes.

Mama Maggie leaned heavily on the table and rose on feeble legs. She pointed to a large wooden cane next to Gwynevere's leg. "Hand me my walking stick, would you, dear?"

"Of course," Gwynevere nodded. She retrieved the gnarled staff and passed it to her grandmother. Gwynevere reeled back in shocked surprise when the old woman grabbed her hands. "Grandmother, what are you doing?!" she cried out. She tried to pull her hands away, but Mama Maggie's grip was unbreakable. "You're hurting me!" Flames erupted from her hands. "Stop!" Gwynevere screamed.

"I am sorry, dear," she said with a heavy sigh. "But I am *not* one to tolerate liars."

"I'm not lying!" The pain was too intense. Gwynevere closed her eyes, and leapt blindly backward, crashing to the floor on her back.

Mama Maggie scoffed at the child writhing in pain. *Wham!* She slammed the cane against the floor. "Of course, you're a dhampir. Sadly, you didn't feel the full effect of the spell," she muttered. "Such a shame. It's splendidly gruesome." She stood overtop of Gwynevere and scowled. "The Academy would have never allowed something like *you* into their fold. Impure. You're a disgrace, sniveling on the floor like an insect. Witches are *pure* and powerful beings—how dare you contaminate magi blood with your vile half-bred blood?"

Samuel squeaked, terrified for his master. *Please, Please. Get up!* he begged. Gwynevere lay on the floor gasping in shock and betrayal. Mama Maggie shook her head and cackled, "Foolish girl." She passed her hand over her face revealing her true appearance.

Gwynevere's mouth fell open. Her teary eyes, filled with confusion, tried to make sense of what was happening. Mama Maggie was no longer a hunched back, grizzled old woman, but a beautiful, youthful sorceress with malice in her eyes. "What's happening?" Gwynevere's voice cracked.

The woman shook her head and smiled, "*Pacificus Mortalis!*" Gwynevere's body stiffened like a board. "Now look what you've made me go and do." Her grandmother's face took on a pout. "No hard feelings, darling."

Gwynevere was paralyzed from the top of her pointed hat to the tip of her toes. Only her eyes seemed unaffected by the spell. She stared wildly at the woman. Was this the end?

Her grandmother made a quick gesture with her hand, causing Gwynevere to slowly rise into the air. She pulled out a large sack, and gently removed her granddaughter's hat. "There, there, so well-behaved." She brushed Gwynevere's hair from her face, leaned in, and kissed her forehead.

"Don't worry, my child. I'll take very good care of you. After all, we're still family." She smiled and yanked the sack over Gwynevere's head.

12 – Storm

Samuel squeaked incessantly as he gnawed through the remaining bit of cord wrapped around the sack covering Gwynevere's head. With one final chomp, he severed the last fibers of the rope. She tried to remove the sack, but she'd just began to get some feeling back in her hands. Samuel repositioned himself, and began tugging, trying to free his master. "Thank you, Samuel!" she cried out, finally able to speak. Samuel squeaked back excitedly, overjoyed that she was okay.

"Gwynevere? Is that you?" came a familiar voice.

"Evelyn?" Gwynevere cried.

"Yes, it's me! Are you okay?!" she called back.

"Yes, no. I mean, I'm not okay, but I'm fine." Samuel gave a mighty tug, finally freeing her. "Thank you, Samuel." The young witch blinked her eyes trying to get her bearings. The room was pitch black and smelled like a stable. She pushed herself up, feeling coarse fabric and hay beneath her fingertips. "Where are we?"

"Some kind of makeshift prison. Father and I were captured," she replied. "We—" A door creaked open, and Evelyn fell silent.

Suddenly, oil lamps—hidden beneath the cloak of darkness—sparked to life, illuminating the room. Gwynevere quickly took in her surroundings—small room, stone walls, except for the one facing a hallway, which was made of iron bars. She could see her sister and Mr. Moody in a cell directly across from her.

There was a soft shuffle of footsteps and then the man—formerly known as Inspector Morgan, now addressed as Chamberlain Morgan—appeared, a look of salacious merriment in his eyes. "So happy to see you girls have awoken. I hope that you found your accommodations relaxing," he chuckled. He rapped his knuckles on the iron bars, the clanging noise echoed in the hallway. "It is regretful we had to go about this in such a way. For that, you have only your sister to blame."

"To blame? Is it wrong to want to find out who killed my mother, and to clear my name?!" Gwynevere yelled.

Morgan shook his head. "Such an outburst is very unladylike. Your mother had many secrets," a wide grin spread across his face, "many that she didn't want you to know."

Gwynevere leapt across the room and slammed into the iron bars. "My mother was poisoned, and my father and I are being blamed. What would you do? Wouldn't you want to clear your name?"

"Adelaide Proctor dabbled in many things, little Merry," said Morgan. His expression darkened into a scowl. "Worst of all, she dabbled with humankind." He spun on his heel and looked directly at Thomas, who sat as if in a trance, staring at his feet.

"How could you say such a horrid thing?!" cried Evelyn. "You made our lives a living hell. My father worked his fingers to the bone to provide for me, to make a life for us, while you pranced around Yorkshire like you owned the place."

"My dear…," he chuckled and shook his head. "I *do* own the place."

Evelyn took a step back in shock. She turned to her father who looked equally confused. Rufus appeared behind Morgan. He slowly rubbed his body along his leg, flicked his tail and then meowed at Evelyn.

Evelyn scowled at her familiar. "Absolutely not! I want nothing of you. You betrayed me and my father."

Morgan knelt and scratched Rufus behind the ears. "You know," he smiled, enjoying the tension of the moment, "you should thank your familiar for hiding the truth from you. I mean, though you weren't behind actual bars, you have been imprisoned your entire life."

"Because of you! You turned the townspeople against us. You tried to destroy my father so he couldn't earn a decent living. We lived in poverty while you dined with the rich!" Evelyn grabbed the bars and rattled them furiously.

"Listen! Listen to me!" Morgan shouted. "I'm going to explain everything. But you must have your wits about you," he tilted his head to Evelyn, and eyed her beneath a cocked eyebrow. "That goes for you as well young lady," he turned to Gwynevere his face stern. Morgan waved his hand, and the cell doors clanged open. "Follow me." He turned with a flourish of his cape and strode down the hallway.

Gwynevere rushed into Evelyn's cell and threw her arms around her sister. "I'm so glad you're okay," she cried. She grabbed her shoulders and gently pushed her away. Her eyes traveled from her feet to the top of her head.

"What are you doing?" Evelyn asked, utterly confused by Gwynevere's behavior.

"I'm checking you for bumps and bruises you loon."

"I'm fine but help me with Father. I guess mortals aren't able to recover from magical spells as quickly as us." Thomas sat on a stack of burlap bags rubbing his swollen red eyes. Gwynevere swallowed the rage she felt inside. Humans truly were frail creatures. Together, with Thomas staggering between them, they stumbled through the hallway and out the door.

"W-wait, what?" Evelyn gasped. "We're in Yorkshire?" She turned back to the building they had just exited—the building she had always known as the city hall. "I-I don't understand." Gwynevere and Mr. Moody looked just as confused.

"Ah," laughed Morgan, "and now you learn the lesson that what you perceive to be true, doesn't mean it's true. Watch," he put his fingers to his mouth and whistled shrilly. Instantly doors flung open, shops came to life, and the streets filled with townsfolk. They all proceeded to go about their day as if nothing had happened. They passed Thomas and the girls without as much as a hello.

Evelyn started to choke up. "What's going on? Hello, Mrs. Roberts!" She called out to a middle-aged woman holding hands with her daughter as they passed by.

"Hello, Evelyn," the woman replied with a smile, "Lovely evening." Her daughter looked up at Evelyn with big blue eyes and smiled. "Is your father still selling shoes? I'm in need of three pairs, one for Caroline and two for my husband." The woman didn't wait for an answer, she lifted her chin and then continued down the street.

Evelyn looked from her father to Mr. Morgan. "What is happening, why is everyone behaving so strangely? Are they under some kind of spell?"

Samuel stood on Gwynevere's shoulder and began squeaking urgently. She sniffed the air and nodded. "They're ghouls, Evelyn."

"Ghouls?" whispered Evelyn, her mouth fell open. It was too much to comprehend.

"Perceptive young lady," chuckled Morgan. "You hit the nail on the head."

"What are ghouls? How do you know they're ghouls?" asked Evelyn.

"I can tell by the smell," Gwynevere explained. "It all makes sense now. Both times I came to this town, I noticed a particular smell, I simply couldn't place it... I thought it was because of the rural environment. But no... I know this smell. The council uses strong scents, like flowers and perfumes to mask the smell of the undead."

Mr. Moody looked like he was going to be sick. The color fled from his face and his lips began to tremble. "They're all... *dead*?"

"It's a little different," Gwynevere replied. "Ghouls are reanimated and given life through the magic of witches and warlocks. They can only listen and obey. They have no free will."

Evelyn shook her head mournfully, watching the townsfolk go about their business. "This is horrible.

You control everything they do?" She looked at Morgan, not even attempting to hide the disgust she felt for the man.

"Stop!" Morgan shouted. Everyone in the town froze. He chuckled at the shocked expressions of the girls and Thomas. "Now you know that I'm telling you the truth."

"You're an evil man," hissed Evelyn.

"Tsk. Tsk. You're such an insolent little thing," he laughed smugly.

"How dare you talk to my daughter like that!" Thomas balled his hands into fists.

Morgan laughed, "Such antics. Oh dear, now I know which side of the family Evelyn inherited her temper."

"Did you just bring us here to gloat?" Gwynevere asked angrily. "To show off? Or is there some meaning behind all of this?"

"More than you realize," came a crackling female voice. Mama Maggie exited the city hall and stood beside Morgan, sizing up the group. Rufus who had been quiet until now, arched his back and hissed at her. She looked down at the cat and scoffed. "Oh, shut up. I promised that no one would be harmed, not that this illusion," she gestured toward the city, "would be kept up forever."

Evelyn looked at Mama Maggie in disbelief. She cocked her head to the side, and turned toward her father, who seemed equally confused. "Miss Bigsby...?" she asked.

"W-wait what?" asked Gwynevere, "She's not Miss Bigsby."

"Of course I am, dear... well to Thomas and his lovely daughter." She approached Evelyn and gently stroked her cheek. "You've really grown into your powers. Imagine, all without proper training or guidance. You've surely moved beyond your mother's ridiculous recipe book."

Evelyn scowled at her and smacked her hand away. Who was this horrid woman who had pretended to be their friend? "Who are you?"

"Magdalyn Proctor," Thomas muttered, "Adelaide's mother," he explained. "Why only now am I recognizing who you are?"

"Because I'm no longer trying to hide myself silly human," she laughed. She grabbed him by the chin, digging her fingers into his cheek. "This is all your fault." She flung him through the air like a rag doll.

"Father!" Evelyn dashed over to her father and helped him to his feet. "Are you okay?"

"I'm fine," he said dusting off the seat of his pants. "You've some nerve, saying this is all my fault when you and Morgan have done nothing but lied and deceived. You're—"

"You're right, dear Thomas," Mama Maggie acknowledged with a chuckle. "I can't lay all the blame on your weak human shoulders, it's just as much Adelaide's fault. However," she pointed a finger at Thomas, "you couldn't tell her the *one* thing she needed to hear, *no*."

Gwynevere couldn't take it anymore. She charged Mama Maggie, but just as her fingers were about to touch her, she crumbled at her feet as if crashing into a brick wall. Samuel lay on the ground beside Gwynevere, squeaking angrily. "I know, I know, I thought it was a good idea," she moaned.

"Enough!" screamed Evelyn. Her body was trembling, her eyes took on an unnatural glow. Thomas grasped her shoulder and began stroking her hair, trying to calm her.

"What did you expect to be the outcome of all this?" asked Thomas, his eyes filled with anger. "Destroy everyone's lives and just think it was going to all turn out okay? You tortured us, stole years of our lives, and all for what?!"

"Please, Mr. Moody. We are not monsters, we're academics," laughed Morgan. "We built this amazing environment to contain and study your daughter. Her magical power is unlike anything that we've seen. But because of her concern for you and your safety, we were able to keep her under control. Truth be told, she is simply too unpredictable and dangerous to teach."

"That being said," smiled Mama Maggie, "if we had the proper leverage," she eyed Thomas, "and her magical levels were maintained through a mixture of potions—"

"And with the proper guidance—"

"I'd be what? Your puppet, is that it?" asked Evelyn.

"No, no, you're so much like your mother. It's your emotions, my dear, that are your weakness. They make you careless and dangerous."

Evelyn inhaled sharply and clenched her jaw. "You two are both fools. As of now your charade is over. You're disgusting and a disgrace to all magical creatures."

"Oh, my dear, right in the heart," Mama Maggie staggered back laughing.

"Mama Maggie, stop! Haven't you done enough damage? What you've done to Evelyn and her father is beyond cruelty."

"Cruelty?" laughed Mama Maggie harshly. "You have no idea how *much* I've suffered knowing both of my grandchildren were half-bloods. It's an absolute travesty. I should have just banished the lot of you."

Tears fell from Evelyn's eyes. She pushed free from her father and closed her eyes, fighting to come to grips with her entire life being one illusion. The ground began to tremble. Mama Maggie's disgusted expression melted from her face into one of uncertainty. Rufus hurried over to Evelyn, meowing earnestly, trying to console her. Dark clouds swirled across the heavens like celestial tumbleweeds. Jagged bolts of lightning flashed across the sky.

Gwynevere stood frozen, transfixed by the magnitude of Evelyn's power. Samuel squeaked loudly, he was having none of this. He raced up her hair and hid beneath her hat.

Evelyn opened her eyes, the iris alive, like a white-hot flame. She raised a trembling finger and pointed it at Morgan. "You evil little man. You wasted my life and my father's life and turned my cat against me." Thunder boomed like a cannon, echoing off the walls of the buildings.

Thomas scooped up Rufus and grabbed Gwynevere's hand. "Hurry, we must take cover!" he shouted.

"No!" shouted Gwynevere. The wind roared. She grabbed the brim of her hat and pulled it down tightly on her head. "I'm not leaving her!" Thomas gave her a look. He realized he wasn't going to change her mind and bolted off to the safety of the town hall.

"See what you've done?! You've created a monster," Morgan hissed at Mama Maggie. A lightning bolt rocketed toward the ground as if flung by Zeus himself. It struck a tree with a crackling boom, splitting it in half. "I hope that you have some sort of contingency for managing your complete and utter failure!"

"You watch your tongue you sniveling coward," Mama Maggie threatened.

"Shut up!" screamed Evelyn. There was another rumble and then another jagged bolt sizzled through the air, striking the ground between Mama Maggie and Morgan. Dirt and debris rained down on them as they crawled away cursing.

Evelyn's hair began to rise into the air. She lifted her hands to the heavens and began whispering in an ancient tongue. The ground heaved and buckled around her. Gwynevere and the conspirators were suddenly launched into the air, hovering several feet off the ground. Thomas clung to the door of the town hall, and Rufus to him.

"Wicked child," Mama Maggie hissed. She clenched her fingers into a fist, and then focusing all her magical powers at Evelyn, she screamed "Dispelliarmus!"

Morgan twisted in the air toward Mama Maggie, "What was that?!" he screamed. "Was that your plan to stop her?"

She didn't reply. She hung helplessly in the air—her face filled with disbelief. The wind increased, trees toppled, and buildings swayed. Thomas clung to the door handle with all his might, as he was lifted from the ground.

Another bolt of lightning arced through the sky, burning its way through Mama Maggie's hat, striking the ground with a flash at her feet. A blood curdling scream escaped her lips. "You're going to kill us all you fool!"

"Evelyn," pleaded Gwynevere, "please stop! You're going to hurt your father!" She grabbed at her hat, holding it firmly on her head, not wanting her familiar to be blown away by the powerful gusts of wind.

"I can't," Evelyn sobbed, "I don't know how." Lightning struck another tree, sending a flaming branch to the ground. The clouds twisted and churned overhead, rain began to fall, stinging their faces.

Gwynevere knew she had to help Evelyn. Her life had all been a lie, it was too much for her heart to handle. She brushed water from her face and pulled the soaked hair from her eyes. She fought with all of her being to move closer to her sister.

"No!" Evelyn screamed when she realized what Gwynevere was trying to do. "No! I don't want to lose you!"

There was another thunderous boom, and then a flash. Morgan cried out terrified. "We're all going to die!"

Gwynevere reached out and grabbed Evelyn's wrist. She screamed as her body jolted. It was like trying to hold onto lightning. Evelyn's flesh was bone cold, but the electrical heat that raced through her, seared Gwynevere's flesh. The young witch closed her eyes, feeling as if her very soul were on fire. "Let go!" Evelyn screamed. "You'll die!" Tears streamed down Evelyn's face.

"I don't care…," Gwynevere cried. "Mother died before we could meet," she said through gritted teeth. "But she made a potion that brought me to you. I don't believe that was an accident." She released Evelyn's wrist and wrapped her arms around her. "I love you, sister," she pulled herself tighter against her. She swayed and her knees buckled.

"No!" Evelyn screamed. "I don't want to lose you!"

"You won't lose me," Gwynevere whispered as darkness crept into the corner of her eyes. "We'll be together forever. That's what Mother wanted, it's what I—" A strange buzzing sound filled her head, then everything went black.

Evelyn stumbled backward, holding her sister's limp body against her. "Gwynevere," she whispered through tears. The wind died to a whisper, the clouds overhead thinned into elongated wisps, revealing a blackened canvas dotted with stars. She knelt gently, laying Gwynevere on the ground.

Evelyn's heart beat fast. She placed her hands on the young witch's cheeks—her skin felt so hot. She concentrated on all the love she felt for her father, her mother, and her sister. Energy bubbled inside of her—when she felt like she could no longer contain it, she released the love into her sister. "Please," Evelyn whispered, "please."

Gwynevere's eyelids flickered and her eyes flew open. She sat up, twisting her head wildly. "I feel horrible," she moaned. Samuel squeaked at her loudly, chastising her for her behavior. "What do you mean I risked my life? Oh Samuel, don't be so dramatic."

Evelyn grabbed her in a hug, tears streaming down her cheeks, "You're alright? You're really alright?"

"Yeah," Gwynevere said, looking at her confused, "I have a bit of heart burn, and… why are they still here?" she asked pointing to Mama Maggie and Morgan. The old witch was looking more like her grandmother and less like Miss Bigsby.

"Evelyn, your powers are truly impressive. I see that I was mistaken to have made you suffer for so long. With the right training—"

"What are you doing?!" Morgan yelled at Mama Maggie. "Are you insane? It's over! She could have killed us, everyone! She is well beyond anything you are prepared to deal with!"

"I'm a sombre witch. What would I be if I didn't recognize someone that has the potential to become great? I understand now, and under my tutelage—"

"Under your tutelage? You've lost your mind, your granddaughter is a sombre suprismo if I've ever seen one, and she's unstable. She'll need someone equal to her abilities to train her."

"And I suppose I'm to leave that to you and your cheap illusions and parlor tricks?"

Evelyn turned to Gwynevere, "What are they talking about? What is a sombre suprismo?"

"Sombre is a witch that has mastered all the various arts of magic. I don't even know half of them," she smiled. "A sombre suprismo is even more powerful—I only know of a couple."

"Evelyn, my dear," Mama Maggie cooed as she floated toward her, "we could do great things, you and I."

Gwynevere positioned herself between them. "Leave her alone you old hag—you've done enough."

Mama Maggie's eyes began to glow. She raised her hand toward Gwynevere, "Die you worthless half-blood." The words had barely escaped her lips when a baleful howl fill the night sky. The curse she was about to utter, died on her lips.

Thomas and Samuel were flung from the steps of the town hall as a pack of werewolves exploded out the front door. He had just enough time to pull Rufus to his chest and scramble backward to safety. "Not again," he whispered as the pack raced toward Morgan, Mama Maggie and the girls.

The snarling beasts circled around Morgan and the old witch, growling with cold stares. "Magdalyn Proctor!" spoke the booming voice of Mayor Wimbly as he descended the steps of the town hall. "All this time, you have been considered a colleague, a friend to the council of Ashen and to the Academy, yet here I stand, in witness to things I'd never imagined. Horrific deeds...."

"Mayor Wimbly," Gwynevere cried out. "Please, don't punish Evelyn or Mr. Moody—they were simply victims, pawns in this horrid affair. I'm the one that left Ashen... I was trying to find out who murdered my mother." Evelyn grabbed her hand. "It's okay," she whispered in her ear.

"Save it, little Merry," said the Mayor. "We'll discuss your behavior when we return to Ashen." He turned to the old witch and sneered. "Magdalyn Proctor, or should I say Miss Bigsby, you're under arrest."

"Arrest?" she cackled. "Under what grounds?"

"Murder," spat Mayor Wimbly. A werewolf placed his massive paw on her shoulder. "The murder of Judge Aiden. Our trackers have followed the scent to this location."

Evelyn gasped and turned to Gwynevere. "The body. We found a body in the cellar. We hid there because it was filled with spices—we hid there after one of your, uhm… people tried to kill us."

The Mayor raised a brow and then pointed to two of his men, "Check it out. Just to be clear, I never sent anyone here to kill you. I sent a rookie werewolf who was supposed to follow up on a lead as to Judge Aiden's whereabouts, the enchantment spell placed over this land was both a curse and a blessing."

"I'll say," interjected Evelyn. "He nearly tore my house down. It'll cost a fortune to repair the damage."

"I'm sorry," said the Mayor, "but Officer Elm truly wasn't himself—the spell placed on this land caused him to turn feral. But, in a moment of lucidity, he was able to realize what had happened in this town, return to Ashen, and report it."

"I'm glad he was able to return back to normal. What Mama Maggie and Morgan did was unfathomable," Evelyn declared.

"And who might you be?" asked the Mayor.

"I'm Evelyn Moody, the child of Thomas Moody and Adelaide Proctor." She pointed to her father who stood at the edge of the circle, still clutching Rufus in his arms. "You know my sister Gwynevere. Oh, and according to that man over there…," she gestured to Morgan who at the moment was being bound in chains by two hulking werewolves, "…I'm a sombre suprismo."

"Is that so?" The Mayor eyed her curiously, then turned to Gwynevere and sighed. "As much as I hate to say this," he paused. "I was wrong to accuse you so quickly. I don't think you had anything to do with the crimes committed. That being said, I'm sure you have *quite* the story to tell between the two of you."

Gwynevere let out a heavy sigh of relief as Samuel popped his head out and brushed some sweat off her brow. "What happens now, Mayor Wimbly?"

"We'll return to Ashen and sort things out." He turned in a circle, stopping at Thomas. For a moment, Thomas's breath caught in his throat—was this man taking his daughter? Mayor Wimbly's eyes softened, "You'll come too, Mr. Moody. A daughter needs her father. Even a human one."

Thomas's knees buckled in relief. "Thank you, sir."

13 - Journey

The trial of Magdalyn Proctor was swift. Anonymous whispers and tips linked her to a series of heinous crimes which spanned several decades. Each count of imprisonment—manipulation and kidnapping humans from the mortal world—sealed her fate. She would be stripped of her magical abilities and imprisoned for the rest of her life.

Morgan received a stiff, yet lighter sentence for his role in deceiving Evelyn and Thomas Moody, corpse-napping and illegal reanimation of ghouls without souls. He too was sent off to prison and stripped of his magical powers.

Judge Aiden was set to be given a proper burial. Gwynevere gave the Mayor the small golden ring she found—still attached to the charred robe the judge had been wearing when she was murdered. The girls found that she'd been exposed to a magical spell that released condensed or bottled sunlight. To a vampire, this spell was lethal. Mama Maggie murdered her when she realized the judge was inquiring into her recent behavior. Her tragic death was going to cast a long-lasting shadow over Mayor Wimbly and the council.

Gwynevere was acquitted of any accusations made toward her as new evidence came to light regarding the passing of Adelaide Proctor. Gwynevere stepped out of the courtroom and rushed into the waiting arms of her sister. Evelyn jumped up and down in excitement. "Guess what?!"

"What?" She tilted her head and snorted at the sight of Mr. Moody, Rufus snuggled in his arms and Samuel sat on his shoulder, a large goofy grin on his face.

"That woman over there," she gestured with her head. "Told Father and I that we've been given a place to stay right here in Ashen!"

"Really?! That's wonderful!"

Evelyn could see a hint of fear in her sister's eyes—she gently grasped her shoulders, "And you're going to live with us," she added.

"Gwynevere," said Dolly softly, "I arranged for everything. I believe it's the best decision considering your father is still at large for the accusations against him. You'll be living in the house I once called home."

"Your home?" Gwynevere looked shocked. "I apologize, Dolly," she held up her hands pleading, "I had no idea that you had a home."

The ghoul laughed and nodded her head. "That is understandable," she said. "I am a ghoul after all, but my soul once was not. I had a beautiful home then, and it is still quite lovely."

"I'm sure," smiled Gwynevere. "Thank you, Dolly, I don't know what to say."

"Think nothing of it," she waved the young witch's comment aside. "I do have one other thing to give you."

Both girls had been eyeing the small rectangular box in her hands—a thatch of letters was tied to the top with a length of string. "This box was left on my desk the morning before your mother passed away. There was a note with it that said to deliver it to you when I thought the time would be right. I feel like there is no better time than the present."

"Thank you, Dolly," said Gwynevere. "For everything."

"I'm going to give you some privacy," Dolly smiled. She turned and waved at Thomas, who awkwardly waved and smiled in return. Gwynevere and Evelyn looked at each other and then burst out in laughter. Though he was just as curious as to the contents of the package, he told the girls that he'd wait for them on a bench across the room.

Gwynevere stared at the box and envelopes quizzically. "What do you think this is all about?" she whispered.

"I have no idea! Should we open it here, or in private?" Evelyn looked around the nearly empty room. Those who were milling around seemed to be in their own little worlds. "Let's sit over there," she gestured to a small wooden bench nestled in the back corner of the room, beneath a picture of a solemn werewolf. "His name is Lord Houndsly," she smiled.

Gwynevere laughed, "Seems appropriate."

Evelyn stole a quick glance at her father. He was stroking Rufus, who was snuggled into his lap. Samuel had fallen asleep on the bench beside him. Thomas's face and shoulders were relaxed. He stared across the room with a vacant expression, but Evelyn knew his mind was churning away—probably thinking about her, and his new life in Ashen. She smiled and turned her attention back to Gwynevere who was holding an envelope with the word 'Urgent' scribbled on it.

Gwynevere opened the letter and blinked. "Uhm, Evelyn, this one has *your* name on it."

"Oh!" Evelyn exclaimed breathily, "It's Mom's handwriting. 'My sweetest Evelyn,'" she read aloud. She paused and breathed out slowly. Tears filled her eyes, and she smiled sweetly. "If you don't mind," said Evelyn, "I'm going to read the letter to myself."

"Yes, please!" Gwynevere exclaimed. She waited patiently as Evelyn cherished each word.

The letter explained to Evelyn that she was indeed a sombre suprismo. A rare type of witch born with a power and capability far beyond that of a sombre witch. She explained that she had left the recipe book with her, in hopes that she would practice and learn on her own. Adelaide also apologized for the hardships that she knew Evelyn would experience and to have patience with her father. It ended with the words, I love you, and I'm so proud of you.

Evelyn turned toward Gwynevere and smiled, "She told me that I'm a sombre suprismo and to be patient with my father." Both girls looked over at Thomas, who was scratching Rufus behind the ears.

Samuel squeaked, leapt from the bench, and scurried across the floor to Gwynevere. She leaned over and scooped him up. He dashed up her arm and sat on her shoulder.

Rufus twitched his ear and stretched. He let out a grumpy meow, jumped lightly to the floor and hurried over to Evelyn, his tail raised in the shape of a question mark. He meowed and deftly leapt onto the bench and settled himself in Evelyn's lap. "Well, you little rascal," laughed Evelyn, "just make yourself at home why don't you?"

"Odd… there's a second letter marked urgent," said Gwynevere.

"Maybe they're all marked urgent," suggested Evelyn, half-joking.

Gwynevere fanned through the others, "I don't believe so, and that would sort of defeat the purpose," she laughed. "Alright," she said, her fingers trembling in anticipation, "let's see what she had to say." Samuel stood, and twitched his nose, watching intently as she unfolded the letter. Gwynevere's eyes watered as she mouthed the words of two different handwritings on her letter.

"It's from Mother and Father," whispered Gwynevere. She brushed a hand across her cheek, wiping away tears. Evelyn smiled gently and rubbed her sister's back. "They're apologizing for fighting, that they both only wanted what was best for me," she continued, then suddenly her mouth dropped open and the letter slid from her fingertips. Evelyn caught it before it fell to the floor.

"What is it? Gwynevere, are you okay?!"

Evelyn clutched the letter and began reading in earnest. "'Please forgive me, I know this has been difficult and I had planned on telling you more, but being out of time, I was forced to take urgent measures.'" Evelyn read aloud. "'The poison I took will still my beating heart… and your father will willingly take the blame. There are dangerous people with sinister agendas in high places. Use all that I have taught you, and you will find your way. I love you Gwynevere and just know this, not all endings are final.'" She looked at her sister, her face twisted in confusion. "She poisoned herself?" she cried. Gwynevere put her finger to her lips and looked around the room making sure they weren't calling too much attention to themselves. "I'm sorry," Evelyn whispered.

"If I understand what she's saying, it's both heart-wrenching and mysteriously wonderful at the same time," Gwynevere said quietly. "Mother knew what Mama Maggie was up to and took the poison to protect us. Remember, my grandmother held a high position at the Academy. Grandma didn't want anyone to find out about you."

"Because my father is human?" asked Evelyn.

"Exactly. Her own daughter, having a child with a human. To Mama Maggie there was nothing worse. So instead, she and Morgan created an elaborate plot to imprison you and keep you tucked away forever. However, I inadvertently foiled their plans when I found a way into your world."

"So, she killed herself?" Evelyn asked in disbelief.

"If she hadn't, Mama Maggie would have. Our mom was the one who sent the anonymous tip that led the werewolves to investigate the fake town. It wouldn't have taken grandmother long to put two and two together and come after her. Plus, it put the police on track of Judge Aiden's murder."

"So... it was Mother who was always hiding in the shadows? I'd catch a flash of movement from time to time." Rufus meowed, looking up at Evelyn, confirming her revelation. She scooped him up and kissed him on the nose. "And of course, you were not allowed to tell me that either." Rufus nodded and meowed. "I understand," she said placing him gently on her lap.

Gwynevere took Evelyn's hand and smiled gently. "Mother was always one step ahead, and I think she drank the poison knowing that she could be revived."

"Wait a minute, Gwynevere!" Evelyn exclaimed, squeezing her sister's hand, "What are you talking about?!"

"The Sanguines Drop. It's an ancient vessel that can preserve the blood of a loved one. It was used in ancient vampire rituals of resurrection. I think Mother is somehow going to use this to revive herself."

Evelyn's eyes grew wide with excitement. "Is that really possible? That would be amazing!" she cried.

Gwynevere smiled and nodded, afraid that it was too good to be true. "I think we should go through the rest of the letters later. There's quite a few, and I believe your father is exhausted." Evelyn followed Gwynevere's gaze. Mr. Moody had stretched out on the bench and was sound asleep.

"He's been through a lot," Evelyn stared at her father affectionately. Gwynevere nodded in agreement. "So, what's next? I feel like we've just begun to scratch the surface."

"Yes, I think—"

"Gwynevere Merry? Evelyn Moody?" A booming voice rang out. Evelyn jumped sending Rufus flying out of her lap. Samuel clung to Gwynevere's shoulder for dear life. A tall slender man with a shiny black cane and a purple flowing cape approached them.

"Yes, sir," the girls chorused, transfixed by the man's massive mustache that hung beneath each nostril like a furry crescent moon.

"Dolly said that I would find you here," he smiled, revealing perfectly white teeth. A tiny bewhiskered pink nose poked its head from between the buttons of his velvet vest. The tiny nostrils flared, then the miniature proboscis disappeared. He chuckled at their confused stares. "I am Headmaster Ozark of the Ashen Academy, and…," he gestured toward his chest, "you just met Wilbert, or," he cocked an eyebrow, "at least his nose."

"Nice to meet you, sir," said Gwynevere leaping to her feet. She wasn't sure if she was supposed to shake his hand, bow or salute. She'd never stood in the presence of such an ominous and imposing figure before. Evelyn rose and stood quietly beside her sister, shifting from foot to foot.

"I'm terribly sorry about your mother. She was a splendid woman and an incredible potion master. There were few that could equal her abilities." He smiled kindly and stroked his magnificent mustache.

"Thank you, Headmaster," said Gwynevere.

"Thank you," Evelyn nodded politely.

"You're certainly welcome. The Mayor and I have spoken at length about the crimes committed, the case of your mother and the disappearance of your father has echoed throughout the realm." He studied the girls for a moment, and then a curious look filled his eyes. "There are many mysterious things afoot, and I'm afraid I simply don't have the resources necessary to follow up on all of these strange occurrences."

Gwynevere and Evelyn looked at each other, then back at the headmaster.

"However, you two have proven most adept at handling yourselves, in shall we say, unconventional circumstances." He cocked an eyebrow and folded his arms across his chest. "I have a hunch that you two may be just what the Academy needs more than ever."

"The Academy?! It would be an honor, sir," gushed Gwynevere.

"I would attend, too?" Evelyn asked.

"I would have it no other way. The Mayor tells me that you have secured a new residence, and that there is no reason why you cannot begin your studies immediately." He looked expectantly at the girls, who both nodded, trembling with excitement.

Headmaster Ozark twitched his moustache and chuckled as he tapped his cane on the ground. "So be it. I look forward to seeing you at the Academy soon."

The girls watched as Headmaster Ozark walked away. Both of them unsure where their journey would take them next, but there was one thing they both knew for sure—they were more than ready.

Evelyn grabbed her sister's hand and leaned her head against hers. "From now on, we'll be together." Rufus meowed in agreement and rubbed himself against Evelyn's leg.

"Forever," Gwynevere beamed, embracing her sister. *Forever*, squeaked Samuel with a twitch of his nose.

Sneak Peek
Bittersweet Deceit
Book 2

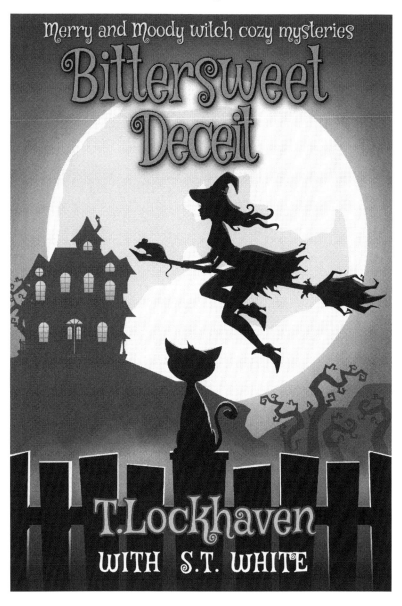

Merry and Moody witch cozy mysteries

Bittersweet Deceit

T.Lockhaven
WITH S.T. WHITE

1 – Raven

The raven cast its shadow over the rolling fields leading into the enchanted forest of Ashen. With a throaty caw, the majestic avian tilted its wings and dipped into the dense trees, its keen eyes focused on a trail of luminescent mushrooms that lit up the dark forest floor. Trees and vegetation flashed by as the raven's powerful wings beat a steady rhythm.

Moments later, it burst from the shadows of the woodland into an open grove that led to a lonely old cottage, nestled into the hillside away from the morning sun. A lonely ranger veiled in a cloak stood on the stoop of the abandoned home. The silhouetted figure's eyes traversed the sky, and raised their arm, granting a perfect place for the raven to perch.

"Welcome back, Brainard. I'm curious my friend," the woman spoke softly, "what did you see?"

"Coast is clear, Meryl," squawked Brainard. He fluttered his wings and adjusted his stance on his master's arm.

"Good," Meryl replied. She affectionately scratched his head. Meryl lifted her own hood, that had fallen over her forehead, revealing eyes with a radiant violet hue and hair so black it shimmered in the sunlight. "This," she gestured to the quaint cottage, "is the place Magdalyn Proctor called home."

Brainard tilted his head and ruffled his feathers. "Danger," he said. "Danger. Caw."

Meryl nodded and breathed out slowly. "I sense it, too. Keep your eyes peeled," she said as she reached out and pressed her palm against the cool, wooden door.

Her hand began to glow. There was a mechanical click, then the door swung open, the large metal hinges screeching the whole way. Meryl paused in the doorway, a rush of stale air greeted her. She took a measured step, placing her boot ever so carefully inside. The loose flooring groaned under the weight of her step. She hesitated, her eyes slowly explored the room, everything seemed to be the way the former sombre witch had left it.

Brainard twitched nervously on Meryl's arm before fluttering up onto the rafters. Even though she knew the house was empty, it felt like an ominous presence still lingered within. She spotted an old cauldron and a table full of empty bottles, many fallen over or shattered on the floor.

"Ransacked, ransacked," squawked Brainard from his perch.

"But the trial wasn't even a week ago," Meryl muttered. "This place has been picked clean." A loud metallic click cut through the silence. She turned and stared at the door. "Magically resealed."

"Suspicious, Meryl, suspicious," spoke the raven familiar.

"You said it," agreed the ranger. She breathed in and released the air slowly through pursed lips, trying to calm her heart. Something about the fireplace caught her attention. Freshly burnt wood. She reached out slowly and touched the ashes with the tip of her fingers. "I sense a magical remnant here." Meryl bit her lip and shuddered at the resonation of magic at her fingertips. Brainard squawked anxiously as he observed his master. Meryl's eyes began to glow, she felt the energy building inside of her. "Show me," she spoke in a soft yet commanding whisper.

Instantly, the logs were consumed by a bright radiant flame. Meryl took several steps back as all the candles that lingered within the barren home lit as well. The events of the past arose like a specter around her. The light of day dissolved into darkness of the previous night.

Meryl removed her hood, letting it fall against the nape of her neck. Her elf-like ears twitched at the sound of a slow, steady hum. Brainard paced and fidgeted atop the rafter, fearing for his master.

A shadow of the past appeared, it knelt beside her, carefully placing papers into the open flame of the fireplace. Meryl stepped closer in an attempt to determine the identity of the shadow. "Hello," she spoke softly. The apparition continued feeding scraps of paper into the flame. She moved closer to the figure and reached out to touch their shoulder, only for the shadow to disintegrate in a cloud of black shimmering dust before her eyes. The magical remnants vanished as the morning sunlight once again, peeked through the windows.

"Curses," Meryl breathed out and furrowed her brow. "Someone was here after Magdalyn Proctor's arrest. They were burning evidence of something. I'm quite sure."

Brainard fluttered his wings. "Careful, Meryl, careful," he squawked.

"But what was that old witch in possession of that someone wanted to keep hidden?" Meryl asked herself. Brainard bobbed his head. "Yeah, me either," she shrugged.

Meryl inspected the fireplace, searching for a scrap of paper that may have escaped. She dropped to her hands and knees, but instead of finding remnants of paper along the cobblestone base, she found droplets of dried blood. She followed the crimson trail from the hearth to the back of the cottage. The blood trail stopped at the seam of a suspicious piece of floorboard.

Brainard eyed the board warily and shuddered. "Careful, Meryl, careful," he squawked.

"I will," she nodded without taking her eyes from the floor. She thrust her hand forward. The secret latch slid aside with a heavy thunk, flinging a trap door open. Brainard flew closer and ruffled his feathers as a wave of putrid heat wafted up from the gaping opening. Meryl staggered back and held her nose in disgust.

"Horrible odor! Horrible odor!" squawked Brainard.

"Thank you, Brainard," Meryl groaned. She held her hand out and created a glowing orb of light. It floated from her hand into the secret cellar. Brainard scrabbled along the rafter and watched safely from above. Meryl crouched, and braced herself on the edge of the opening. The stench was unbearable. The orb of light revealed a ladder and a large barren room. Perhaps, thought Meryl, it runs the entire length of the house. She motioned for the light to move further into the room. "What is that?" she whispered.

The light hovered in the air, revealing faint, indecipherable, writing on the coarse stone wall. She furrowed her brow, concentrating on the strangely familiar shapes. It was when she blinked that she noticed something at the edge of the shadows. She waved her hand to make the sphere glow brighter.

Meryl gasped. It was the robed figure from the vision. Their body was twisted in an unnatural position, surrounded in a pool of dried blood. Meryl screamed and yanked her head out of the basement. Her eyes flashed a vibrant violet. "Show me more," she whispered in an attempt to trigger the lingering remnants of magic within the house.

Screams filled the air around her. There was the sound of a struggle and then muffled whimpers. A heavy thud shook the room, causing Meryl to jump. She thrust her hand out toward the shadows moving in front of her.

"Fire!" shrieked Brainard. "Fire!"

"What?"

The raven's shrill cry and the searing pain brought her out of her trance. In her stupor, she'd thrust her hand into the fireplace. Flames hungrily consumed the cloth of her sleeve, licking at her clenched fist. She blew the fire out with a wave of her hand.

Brainard danced on the rafter in a panic. "Caw! You lost yourself!"

Meryl shivered in the darkness, she could feel the wickedness, like icy cold fingers encircling her neck. "So much evil lingers here," she whispered with a heavy sigh. She uncurled her fingers and stared—a charred, splintered timber with a distinct engraving of a blood droplet carved within, rested on her palm. The symbol began to glow, and then like a dying flame, flickered out.

Meryl turned toward Brainard and held out her arm to him. "Come my friend. We must report this to the headmaster at once."

Gwynevere woke to the calamitous sound of picture frames vibrating across her chest of drawers. She rubbed her tired eyes and caught her alarm clock as it crept toward the edge of her nightstand. "Evelyn!" she called out. "You're doing it again!" She could see her sister twisting and twitching in her sleep across the room. Her cat, Rufus, seemed oblivious to her gesticulations as he rested peacefully on her chest. "Evelyn!" Gwynevere said a little more forcefully, "Are you having another nightmare?"

The young dhampir's hand shot out catching a book as it fell with her lightning-fast reflexes.

"AGH!" snorted Evelyn. She shot up in a cold sweat, flinging a surprised Rufus into the air. He growled angrily midflight, landing gracefully on all fours. He turned and meowed loudly to Evelyn, his hair standing on end.

"Someone's in trouble," snickered Gwynevere.

Evelyn gasped and wiped the drool from her mouth with the sleeve of her nightshirt. She brushed her hair back and rubbed the sweat on her neck.

"Good morning, sunshine," she snapped her fingers, magically drawing back the curtains to light up the room. "Did you have a bad dream?"

Evelyn surveyed the room—pictures hung cockeyed on the wall, books on their sides. She eyed her sister through a sleep haze. "Sorry about that."

Gwynevere smiled back before hopping out of bed and hurrying over to her. Her bare feet skittered across the cold floor as she jumped into Evelyn's bed. "You never need to apologize, your talents may come in handy should we decide to redecorate the room," she said as she grabbed the blankets and wrapped them around both her and her sister.

"Funny…," said Evelyn rolling her eyes. She cuddled up to her, gently laying her head against her shoulder. "Your feet are freezing."

"I know, I'm cold-blooded." Gwynevere raised a mischievous eyebrow, then placed her ice-cold feet on her sister's legs.

Evelyn gasped as she pushed her feet off of her. "You're evil is what you are," she laughed lightheartedly. "Go back to Samuel, I'm sure he misses you over there."

Samuel poked his little white furry head out from beneath the covers of Gwynevere's bed. The rat familiar twitched his nose and gave a defiant squeak, before burrowing back under the blankets.

"Something tells me that's a no," she smirked.

Evelyn sighed and leaned on her sister. "You really are cold though," she said. "What's it like?"

Gwynevere looked at her and shrugged. "I'm not sure I know how to answer that. I've always been like this so…."

"Yeah, makes sense, I never really thought of it that way," Evelyn nodded.

"And other than these," she chomped her teeth together, revealing her razor-sharp fangs, "I'm no different than you."

"I'm curious… if you bit me, would I become a vampire? No, right? Because mom was a witch not a vampire."

Gwynevere looked at her sister and laughed. "Why would I bite you?" she asked. "And no, you wouldn't turn into a vampire, it would just hurt really, really bad."

There was a soft knock at the bedroom door, and then the voice of Thomas Moody, Evelyn's father. "Girls, are you up?" He didn't wait for a response. "That friendly undead woman from the city council brought breakfast."

"We're up, Dad," shouted Evelyn. "We'll be right there."

"I hope Dolly made blood yoke quiche," said Gwynevere excitedly.

Evelyn wrinkled her nose at the thought of such a thing. Samuel hopped off the bed with equal excitement, scurrying out the door behind Gwynevere. Evelyn sighed and smiled softly, soaking in the moment—she no longer had to wake up alone, she had a sister. For so long it had just been her and her father. She slipped from beneath the covers into a pair of slippers and padded across the room. From the doorway, she could see her father helping Dolly—the undead maiden—fill their table with a small feast.

"Oh, wow," she muttered with wide eyes. "She really did bring us a whole breakfast."

"It smells incredible," said Gwynevere. She circled the table placing plates and silverware in front of each chair. Samuel's eyes glazed over. He swayed precariously on Gwynevere's shoulder, hypnotized by the delectable aroma of all the food.

Evelyn rubbed her eyes and attempted to finger comb her bed head. "Good morning everyone," she yawned.

"And a good morning to you, Miss Moody," Dolly chirped with a gleeful grin. "A pleasure to see you and your family adjusting well to your new home."

Gwynevere looked at the ghoul and smiled, her keen eyes noticing that Dolly took the time to straighten her straw-like hair and clip it back with a beaded flower clip. Thomas had even combed his hair. He hummed happily as he pulled the chairs out for everyone.

"Freshly baked bread, corn hash, black pudding, fresh milk, red... quiche?" said Thomas as he named off everything on the table. "This is... a very kind gesture, Miss uh...."

"West," said Dolly as she squeezed her hand and stood patiently for him to try it. "My name in life was Dorothy Alistair, but you can just call me Dolly, dear. Everyone does."

"Thank you so much, Dolly," Thomas shook his head, still overwhelmed by her kindness. "You've already provided us with such a nice place to stay, and now all of this," he gestured at the small table, barely able to contain all the food. "I don't know how to thank you."

"No need to thank me, Mr. Moody. It's my duty after all," said Dolly. She tilted her head ever so slightly and curtsied. She turned and smiled affectionately at the girls, then made her way toward the door. "I must return to work now. Please enjoy."

"Thank you, Dolly," beamed Gwynevere. "You're the absolute best."

"Yes, thank you," said Evelyn.

Thomas pushed away from the table. "Dolly... are you sure you don't want to stay and enjoy this with us?"

Dolly stood at the threshold and paused. A sad smile spread across her face—she felt moved by such a kind gesture. "Thank you, sir, but I simply cannot." Her voice seemed fragile yet heavy. "I only wish to serve your needs, Merry and Moody family."

She quickly turned and closed the door behind her, leaving Thomas standing in awkward silence at the table. He turned and looked at the girls, his face showing his confusion. "Was it something I said?" he asked.

"No, the Mayor keeps Dolly really busy. Too busy in my opinion. And," explained Gwynevere, "since she is a ghoul, she doesn't need to eat or drink."

"Oh," said Thomas, sliding back into his chair. He eyed the table filled with food. It had been a long time since he had been able to provide Evelyn with such a meal. "Of course," he said softly.

Rufus padded lazily into the kitchen, announcing his presence with a series of meows. He brushed his body against Evelyn's legs and then plopped to the ground at her feet.

"Good morning, Rufus." She grabbed a small plate and filled it with black pudding and eggs for her familiar. He thanked her with a heavy dose of purring as he dug right in.

Samuel pulled at Gwynevere's silvery white hair squeaking. "Okay, okay," she sighed. "A little patience." She slid a tiny plate beside her own and filled it with eggs and corn hash. Samuel scurried down her arm squeaking excitedly, as she placed the plate on the floor.

For quite some time, the only sound was the scraping of forks on plates. Gwynevere watched her new family enjoying their meal. She was well aware that both Thomas and Evelyn had a lot to learn about life in Ashen. It had only been three days since they moved into Dolly's unoccupied home after the trial of Gwynevere's grandmother, Mama Maggie. Thomas seemed distant. His mind was clearly elsewhere—even as the family was coming together for their first real meal in days.

"It sure beats bread and soup, right?" smiled Gwynevere between bites, trying to bring life back to the table.

"Yes. Yes. Where are my manners?" said Thomas, shaking his head. "I'm sorry, Gwynevere. I got lost in my own head for a moment."

"It's okay," Gwynevere smiled affectionately at him. "It's a lot to take in. Give it some time."

"I had another nightmare," said Evelyn as she began sampling the quiche.

"I know," said Thomas. He took a sip from his glass of milk and pointed to a picture hanging cockeyed on the wall. "It felt like an earthquake."

Gwynevere looked at the two of them and sat her fork down. "Mr. Moody, do you think it would be okay if I took Evelyn into the city today? You know, to do a little exploring?"

Evelyn's eyes slid from Gwynevere to her father—he wasn't big on exploring. He wiped his mouth with a napkin, wriggled his nose and nodded. "Well... I think Evelyn is old enough to make her own decisions on the matter." He smiled at Evelyn, in a way he hadn't in years. It was as if her father was finding himself again. "The last thing I want you to do is coop yourself up inside the house because of me."

"I know," said Evelyn. "It's just that things are so different here. I have to admit, I'm a little scared of going out there."

"I understand," nodded Gwynevere, "however, we have to face our fears. We can't just keep sitting here waiting for the Academy to come talk to us again. It was unheard of for Headmaster Ozark to approach us like he did. That is a rare opportunity. It's not every single day you get invited to the Academy for tea." She tilted her head and met Evelyn's eyes.

"They said they would be in contact with us when they learned something new about our mother's case."

"So, you would rather sit here? Opportunity has already knocked, I'm not confident that it's going to knock twice."

"It has been a while," Evelyn agreed.

"Almost a week," Gwynevere replied. "Too long in my opinion."

"Too long!" squawked the shrill voice of a raven as it alighted onto a rafter above the table.

Both Evelyn and Gwynevere jumped in their seats. Thomas flung his fork across the kitchen and shot backward in his chair. "Where did that bird come from?!" he gasped.

Rufus looked up at the familiar and hissed. The raven tilted his head and fluttered his wings. Samuel raced up Gwynevere's leg to her lap, squeaking the entire way. "Oh," said Gwynevere. "The Academy?" Samuel nodded.

She jumped up from the table. "Evelyn! They're summoning us to the Academy!"

"Oh!" said Evelyn, her voice filled with excitement. "Is that okay, Father?"

Thomas looked at her and just shook his head and chuckled. "Yes, yes, go."

Evelyn reached across the table, snatched up a piece of bread and stuffed it in her mouth. Gwynevere had already bolted from the table. There was a screech from the kitchen, and then the hurried sound of slippers racing down the hallway. Evelyn slammed the bedroom door, leaving Thomas alone at the table with the three familiars. He glanced at Rufus and Samuel, who seemed to be staring him down. "So," he cleared his throat. "A friend of yours?" he asked, feeling a little silly talking to a rat.

Samuel twitched his whiskers and puffed out his furry chest as both girls burst out of the bedroom. "Bye, Daddy," Evelyn waved with a smile.

"Bye, Mr. Moody," said Gwynevere with a tilt of her mother's pointy hat. She paused for a moment as Samuel leapt off the table, slid across the floor, then scrambled up her leg, over her dress and settled into her hat.

Thomas whirled in his seat, "That was fast," he said, trying to comprehend how they changed their clothes so quickly.

"A proper witch must always be ready at the blink of an eye," said Gwynevere with a playful wink. She pushed the door open and glanced up at the raven. "Come on!"

Evelyn who was already waiting on the front stoop, turned into the doorway and patted her thighs. Rufus meowed and yawned, letting out one more good stretch before padding across the room and leaping into Evelyn's arms. She smiled, her heart filled with excitement. She was nervous, but excited to embrace the new city, and a new adventure. She locked hands with her sister as they followed the mysterious raven through the bustling streets of Ashen to their destination, the prestigious Ashen Academy.

More from T. Lockhaven

We hope you enjoyed reading *Potion Commotion*, the first book in *Merry and Moody Witch Cozy Mysteries* series. Let us know what you think by leaving a review on Amazon, Barnes & Noble and/or Goodreads. Thank you so very much!

Follow T. Lockhaven's author page on Amazon or on Goodreads for new release updates and giveaways.

Other cozy mysteries by T. Lockhaven

The Coffee House Sleuths

Book 1: A Garden to Die For
Book 2: A Mummy to Die For
Upcoming: A Role to Die For
Upcoming: A Voyage to Die For

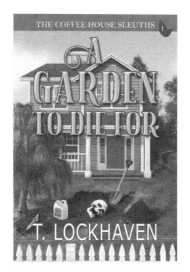

Also written in the series is *Sleighed*, the first book in *The Coffee House Sleuths: A Christmas Cozy Mystery*. *Sleighed* takes place in the same town, with the same characters, but was written as a fun standalone Christmas story.

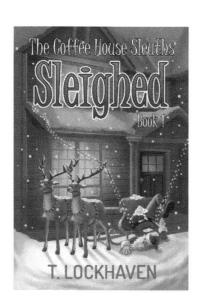

Thomas Lockhaven

T. Lockhaven is also a children's author under the name Thomas Lockhaven, you may find his other works through the following links:

Quest Chasers (Ongoing Series)
Book 1: The Deadly Cavern
Book 2: The Screaming Mummy

Ava & Carol Detective Agency (Ongoing Series)
Book 1: The Mystery of the Pharaoh's Diamonds
Book 2: The Mystery of Solomon's Ring
Book 3: The Haunted Mansion
Book 4: Dognapped
Book 5: The Eye of God
Book 6: The Crown Jewels Mystery
Book 7: The Curse of the Red Devil

Book 8: The Witch's Secret
Book 9: The Christmas Thief

Calista Chase Time Sleuth (Ongoing Series)
Book 1: Blackbeard's Treasure

The Ghosts of Ian Stanley (Ongoing Series)

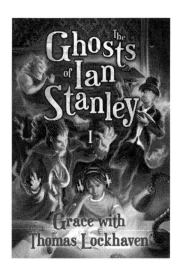

Made in the USA
Middletown, DE
03 February 2022